# CATASTROPHIC EXPECTATIONS:

## *Sex, Love & the Pursuit of Marriage*

# CATASTROPHIC EXPECTATIONS:

## *Sex, Love & the Pursuit of Marriage*

Ellen Marie Francisco

THE PERMANENT PRESS
*Sag Harbor, NY 11963*

For information, address:
The Permanent Press
4170 Noyac Road
Sag Harbor, NY 11963
www.thepermanentpress.com

*Library of Congress Cataloging-in-Publication Data*

Francisco, Ellen Marie, author.
Title: Catastrophic expectations: sex, love, & the pursuit of marriage / Ellen Marie Francisco.
Description: Sag Harbor, NY: The Permanent Press, [2020]
ISBN: 978-1-57962-639-6 (cloth)
1. Love stories.

PR9199.4.F734 C38 2020
813'.6—dc23 2020030206

Printed in the United States of America

*To all the men who've come and gone and circled around again.*
*I love you all.*

# Prologue

I've always loved food. Eaten it every day in fact for as long as I can remember. I like playing with it. Now that I think of it, that's probably where it all began—with mud pies as a child. I was an only child. Luckily I had neighborhood playmates like Sheila to play with. She loved to make mud pies. She put everyday garden variety mud in hers, adding water from the garden hose to make it the right consistency. She'd put it into the aluminum pie plate she'd swiped from her mother's kitchen then use more water to give it a smooth top. Sheila finished hers long before I even found the insides for mine. I preferred mud casseroles. They were more time consuming, yes, but entirely worth the effort.

Worms and slugs were my filling, and sometimes even seeds Mother planned on using to grow vegetables in our own backyard garden. Sheila squealed when I used my bare hands to free a worm from the earth. I'd hold it up to her and wiggle it some more between my fingers. She'd squeal louder and start to squirm herself. Then I'd put it in my casserole, a layer of mud there already. Happy.

It's not surprising I decided to become a caterer. There was never any doubt I wanted to work with food. If the home-economics teacher hadn't seen my latent talent and steered me in the right direction by suggesting culinary school, I might have been content to become a homemaker. I whizzed through all our cooking classes.

You might think Mother was a cook extraordinaire and I learned from her. Not even close to the truth. The fact is she was a terrible cook, and while she flubbed her way through macaroni and cheese and store-bought frozen entrées during my most formative years, my innate wisdom told me even then, there was more to dinner than that. I was born with taste.

When I was old enough to manage being home alone after school, Mother reentered the work force. I was assigned to cooking. At first it was merely taking the Chef Express package from the freezer, peeling its protective wrapping, and emptying the contents onto a foil-lined baking sheet. (Neither one of us wanted to wash the baking sheet.) Oven at 350 degrees for twenty minutes. No biggie. I read it off the back of the package.

Several weeks after my assignment as resident cook for my mom and dad, Mother took me to the grocery store and let me pick out some of the Chef Express from the freezer aisle for myself.

"All women should know how to cook," was father's input. Several years later I realized it was a dig at Mother. Certainly he wouldn't think warming trays of Chef Express was cooking?

My experimentation had begun. It continued when I joined the Chef Apprentice School of the Arts. I put my trust into the hands of professionals and learned to work with my own hands. I started my catering business in the tiny kitchen in my apartment and continued to experiment with my *let's see what happens if I do this* attitude. I was born with the nerve to try anything once and blessed with a good business sense.

Some would say I'm married to my work. I built a small and loyal clientele—enough to justify a move into a silver, commercialized kitchen space, and made the transition seamlessly. My clients loved me. I've collected enough brownie points to be on a sugar high until the end of time.

My kitchen is in West Los Angeles, so close to Century City and all the high-rise buildings filled with businesses, it was a no-brainer to go after those hungry executives who don't have time to go out. Last year I packed up a cooler on wheels full of gourmet sandwiches and salads, and my killer brownies wrapped beautifully with my fold-out menu and hustled my way from floor to floor, up and up the elevator until the cooler was empty. I knew I'd have them hooked after just one bite.

A week later calls started to come in and I had to hire a support staff. It took no time at all to become a staple in the community. Before we knew it, we were doing corporate meetings, corporate picnics and everyone was hungry for more.

The five years I've been running my catering company, Lip Service, have been some of my most fulfilling yet. We're getting busier too.

Anyway, it is the weekend, my first off in a while, and I have time enough to ponder this all. I'll flip through my growing collection of cookbooks and mark the pages I may want to come back to. And I'll wonder why I'm doing this all alone.

# Chapter One

## Bratton Mother's Day Brunch

Menu for 20
Made-to-order Omelet Bar
Custard French Toast with Warm Blueberry Compote
Cold Buffet with Bagels & Cream Cheese, Lox, Tomato, Onion & Lemon Caper Garnish
Country Rustic Lemon Poppyseed & Mixed Berry Scones
Mini Apple Cinnamon Muffins

By the time Monday comes around, I'm in the mood for a big fat juicy job. I have the Mother's Day brunch and some other small corporate lunches that are our bread and butter, but I'm dreaming of bigger parties in bigger venues.

When I get to the kitchen, my right-hand gal, Georgina, is in full swing. Hair back. Apron on. She's stamping red lips onto the boxes we use for corporate lunches. I've just crossed the doorway into my office and dropped my keys on the desk when she says, "I'm going to let the ink dry on these boxes before I pack them, okay?" She's got one of our branded Lip Service aprons on. It's got lips all over it too.

"I can help you pack them when they're ready. Are there any messages on the machine?"

"It's been beeping for an hour already," Georgina responds.

Then the red lip-shaped office phone starts to ring like it can't wait to talk. I lunge for the phone.

"Can you hear that, Georgina? I swear the phone rings differently for big jobs. Hear how it's different?" I ask, my ear perked. She looks at me pointedly. She doesn't believe me.

"Lip Service, how may I help you?" I ooze, the telephone firmly against my ear. I am hyped, and in the mood to land another job.

I recognize Shelly Van Buren's voice immediately, a soft lilting cadence, not too loud, not too soft. I've been courting her for a week already. I want to do her engagement party and her wedding and every party she's planning right up until her big day and beyond. "Hi, Gwen, Adam and I have decided we'd like to go ahead and book you for our engagement party. I wanted to discuss the menu if you have time and find out how much of it you make yourself."

"Oh, I don't make food," I say through the line, the saleswoman in me in full force, "I channel it. I have a direct connection to the food gods."

"I've eaten your food. I might just believe that."

"My hands are my facilitators. The energy just flows from me," I say, exaggeratedly. "To say I cook with my heart is an understatement. If you ever saw *Like Water for Chocolate*, you'd know what I mean."

She laughs. "Saw it and read it."

"Well, I don't make people sad. I make them very, very happy."

"I tried one of the recipes at the back of the book. It didn't work for me. I'm not very good."

"That's where I come in."

"Well, we've decided to let you do it because your food was some of the best we've ever tasted."

"Stick with me. You'll never go hungry again. How many of you are there?"

"There are fifty-five."

"Let me put something together for you. I am going to make you so happy." I was nothing if not convincing.

"I want chicken. Lots and lots of chicken."

"You can have it."

"A little meat but not much. Some of my guests won't eat it at all. Californians. I swear they think meat is a bad word. I'm from Texas. What's a meal without it?"

"I know. Believe me. California Cuisine has swept the nation. Chickens are practically flying around here. No problem."

I finish scratching notes while we talk, then end the call.

"I got Van Buren," I proclaim to Georgina, victorious.

"Lips, lips, everywhere. All hail to the lips and every hungry mouth out there. They're going to get their fill, Georgina."

I dial my food rep, Nadine, immediately.

"All right, Nadine, tell me what you've got in the way of fully prepared chicken. I need to just throw it in the oven. I'm in a bit of a hurry on this one. I was thinking appetizers, full breasts for entrées, maybe some drumettes."

"I recommend the Chicken Zings. Even the Chicken Dings are—well, I can't even tell you how good they are. And they're on sale this week."

"What's the difference between the Zings and the Dings?"

"The Zings have more zing. They're spicier."

*!!***!!***!!*

I DECIDE to go with Georgina to help serve the Mother's Day Brunch. I need to get out of the kitchen and clients are so impressed when the boss shows up. I'm secretly hoping there will be a man for me there. Hoping, hoping, hoping. Not that I'm sure I need a man, but last weekend's pondering left me in a wanting state, so I am willing to keep an open mind.

We drive up Pacific Coast Highway in the Lip-Mobile, our converted postal delivery truck painted white with red kisses. It is an eye-catching, lip-smacking attention-grabbing experience for sure. A business card on wheels. We're driving the business in from all over town.

It is a sunny, mothering kind of day, and we enjoy the drive over. As soon as we hit PCH, both of us slide our doors back so we can feel the ocean breeze. I never tire of seeing palm trees and beach and smelling the ocean's salty air. Someone honks at us as I change lanes. Hopefully they are responding to our *honk if you're a foodie* moniker on the back.

My clients, Karl and Kathy Bratton, are hidden somewhere in the house when we arrive with our take-charge attitude. Several trips from the car to the kitchen are needed to get everything together and we work silently, efficiently, like ants on a picnic blanket. Our aprons are on when we hear Kathy Bratton. She appears from a long corridor and greets us graciously, her skin looking freshly pink against a peach bathrobe.

"We had a late night, the two of us, so we'll be awhile yet. I can't tell you where the boys are, but don't let them eat anything if they find you. I want them to sit at the table like cultured humans. My big brother, Jack, is here already. Somewhere. He's got the appetite of five of us so don't even let him into the kitchen until everyone is here. If you need anything, just holler or search for yourself." With that she disappears down the hall.

Her husband, Karl, appears thirty minutes later when Georgina and I are ready to cook. The ingredients for our omelets lie in small bowls surrounding the burner, nonstick cooking spray at the ready, two spatulas placed knowingly beside the nonstick fry pan.

Karl is wearing nylon sweatpants and sneakers. By the look of him he's just been jogging the neighborhood. His exposed torso is glistening with sweat. I have to fight off a vision of what he and Kathy were doing together on their late night. He looks at the counter we've set the buffet on. He examines our platters of bagels and plates with garnish, the french toast and warm blueberry compote I am just finishing up, my mini muffins and scones in a napkin-lined basket. "I don't think you're going to have enough food," he blurts out.

Georgina stops pouring the orange juice and champagne Kathy requested at the last minute. If you must know the truth,

I'm never sure whether there will be enough food. Bad enough that I trip myself up over it—silently in the tortured confines of my own mind—let alone have my client predict I won't have enough and I'm doomed to fail. It's just bad business.

"Well, of course we will," Georgina and I both chime.

We've worked enough side by side to be able to do this. Hail to the power of numbers. I draw his attention to the expansive array of ingredients on the omelet bar and assure him we'll have plenty and even have some leftovers. He seems to buy it. He smiles and leaves us alone in the kitchen, grabbing a banana from their oversized fruit bowl as he is leaving. I tell myself I've never run out before, soothing my inner mind. When he's long gone, I mention it out loud to Georgina. I also imagine he's impotent. A thought I can't fight off.

"Georgina, tell me you think we have enough. We do, don't we?"

"Well, it's only twenty people. Five hungry men, one of them with the appetite of five, I guess, some weight-conscious women, kids. At least five kids, right?"

We look at the food and do the math.

"We'll be fine," we chime.

It's unanimous. We have enough and we'll be fine. All appetites considered. Just to make sure, I rummage through their refrigerator for backup. I find tomatoes, cream cheese, strawberries, and a honeydew melon. I slice and scoop as necessary and lay it all out on platters before the guests arrive. Karl and Kathy are none the wiser.

We meet the mothers, a couple grandmothers, the sisters, and their offspring. The husbands are in their own world across the room. And then there's Jack. Lone wolf in the pack.

They all seem to have a spinach consciousness. Everybody wants it in their omelets, even Jack. He hovers around the island as I work, watching me sauté the spinach and tomato for his mother's Greek omelet. He comes very close to me as I fumble with the feta. He touches my shoulders and introduces himself.

"Hi, I'm Jack. Kathy's brother."

"I have to warn you my spatula has a sharp edge and is oily from butter."

Georgina cuts me a look from the buffet that says she could easily handle this without me. She has so many faces, all of them pretty, no matter the mood behind them, but I know what she's implying, and it isn't pretty.

"Can I get on the list for one of those?"

"Definitely," both Georgina and I chime.

Jack steps away, naming the ingredients he wants in his omelet. He comes back for a second one. He hovers with small talk when he returns for more. I give him a clean plate with two slices of french toast, a slathering of warm blueberry compote, a squirt of whipped cream, a dash of cinnamon. I have to admit my nervousness. He eats it silently, deliberating on every bite. Such an appetite.

"Where's your kitchen?" he asks. "I'd like to come and have dinner with you."

"That's a little nervy of you," I tell him, and "you have it all wrong. Since I made you breakfast, you should take me out for dinner."

"I can bring dinner in hand."

"So, what, I'm providing the wine?"

"I have two hands."

"Well, we'll have to talk about that another time."

Later when all the guests are sufficiently satiated and the kids go off to play, Georgina and I clean up, pleased that we've had enough. I make a show of asking Karl how he'd like the leftovers wrapped. Jack hovers asking inconsequential questions I will not answer. That's the best I can do at playing hard to get.

I'm not even sure how we end up in the Jack and Jill two-door bathroom down the hall. I guess he's Jack and I'm Jill and before I know it, he has his hands on the hills of my chest and then the grass of my pubes. He props me up on the vanity top and unzips his fly. Jack Jr. isn't so junior.

# Chapter Two

## Van Buren Engagement Party

Tray-passed Hors d'Oeuvres Menu for 55
Skewered Grilled Honey Citrus Chicken
Spicy Chicken Zings
Skewered Russian Sweet & Sour Meatballs w/Dipping Sauce
Skewered Jumbo Tortellini Rounds w/Pesto Dipping Sauce
Crab Salad on Endive Leaves

Georgina is concerned I never get out and urges me constantly to date, but I have been soured—as in sucking on a lemon soured—by love. I'm too involved in my career now to care. She persists annoyingly, "It's a big world, why be alone?"

Had I not just had two weekends full of wanting, I might have hushed her already. She has a friend, who has a friend who joined a matchmaking agency, and is engaged after only six or seven dates. We're just about to eat lunch. I've already pulled the barstools over.

"She found her dream man," she tells me. "He joined because he was ready—that's usually the problem with most great men anyway, they're just not ready and no matter how perfect you are, it never goes anywhere."

"News flash," I say. "I don't need a man to take care of me. I'm managing fine myself. I don't need a relationship because I'm needy. It's not like I'm screaming *help me, help me, I'm a damsel in this dress*. Swoon for me. Protect me. Buffer me from the big bad world out there."

"Yeah, you're one tough cookie, Gwen." Again with her looks.

"I'm not. I'm just independent. How about being with someone because I want to and love to—not need to and have to—there's a new slant. I don't want to entangle myself with anyone."

"Yeah. Right." Her underwhelm makes me nervous. That and she's usually right.

I remember we need plates for our lunch and implemental eating devices. I dodge her to get them. Barely back with our plates, she's at it again. I'm in a pressure cooker here and the lid's about to snap on.

"I just want you to get out there socially, find a keeper. Round out your life a little."

"I just want to eat a small sampling of the engagement party menu already waiting for my mouth, Georgina. I want to make sure it all blends well on my picky palette before finalizing our choices. All this talk is going to affect my taste buds."

"You cannot keep going like this. All work, work, work. As much as I appreciate it."

"Yeah, we're on a roll, and on a deadline."

"Just try it for a few months, what's the harm?" she persists convincingly. "You cook. Who cooks nowadays? Really. I'm not kidding. You should do it. Even Philip thinks you should."

She is so convincing I think I must be crazy if not willing to try. I agree to try it. I have to swear in fact. Really! She makes me put my right hand up and left hand over my heart and, I'm not joking, I have to repeat after her, "I, Gwen, do solemnly swear I will join Great Expectations to get a man and try to live happily ever after."

"Finally." We've nearly finished what's left of our lunch. She particularly likes the Chicken Zings. "They're spicy." She's reaching for water and an endive leaf to cool her mouth. "You promised, remember," she says, depositing her napkin in the trash.

"Yeah, yeah. I'm already planning my wedding." Although I'm so not.

Georgina gives me a look as I'm grabbing our empty plates. She has a lot of looks for a girl who thinks she minds her own business. She has her own silent opinion, the raised eyebrows, the crinkled forehead. I want to warn her that one day her face will stay like that, and her silence will forever be displayed for all to see. But I prefer to mind my own business momentarily, and let it go. I've got plenty to think about.

A visual flashback of the bathroom at the Bratton brunch suspends me in time long enough to forget what I am doing. Georgina already suspects something happened at that brunch. She'd be disgusted if I had a case of tell-all and told her what I'd done with Jack in the bathroom. I am warm from my thoughts of him. No, I'm not tellin' nobody.

*!!***!!***!!*

INTENT ON the television set in our kitchen, Georgina and I are food network addicts. It is soothing to know that during the height of our food prep madness, Sara Moulton and Martha Stewart are right there with us. Sometimes we can't even hear them above the hum of our mixers and noisy kitchen gadgets, but just seeing them flash across the screen between shots of food gives us that added bit of reserve needed to get through our workday. *Cooking Live* is just about to come on, and I'm not prepared to miss it. *Sara, Sara, she's our girl*, I hum, turning up the volume.

When I'm in my kitchen I think myself rather conventional. But today I question the context of conventional in my life. Conventional because I work for a living—that I haven't found an unconventional way of becoming independently wealthy. I am stringing my days, weeks, and months—now years—together going from one job to the next, always needing to do the next for the money, so my desires, and wants are strung along with me.

As a child I wanted to break out of myself—to ooze from my own self-inflicted borders. It seemed everyone wanted me to stay within the lines. Why, I wondered, even as a child? Why? What would happen to me? Would I be labeled different? Passionately rebellious? Did I care? I thought not. Somewhere I shied away from standing out—even from wanting to stand out, and yet I had been dying to get out all along.

As a teen I rebelled against my own body changes by becoming a tomboy, and then when the urge struck, I fell into my own willing promiscuity. I'd known all the boys. I was their gal pal and got an inside look at who they really were, a view my female classmates were not privy to.

If I were still a child—locked forever in child land—I would no doubt be coloring in the lines by now, but for sure I'd be the one drawing the lines in the first place.

I have chosen a conventional profession and turned it slightly nonconventional. Sure, I feel elated with the challenge of a job to come. The skill required to cater an engagement party is very different from that needed to host a backyard barbecue, so I keep fresh by constantly having to adapt my services to the changing needs of my clientele. Sure, I reach beyond the lines a bit when I couple certain foods together.

My goal is to stun my clients into a new taste sensation with my, *aren't I something* attitude, but I have learned, known innately all along perhaps, how to do this acceptingly in a palate-pleasing way.

My real unconventional streak manifests in other subtleties—spawned through my latent sexual desires, sufficiently squelched until my recent tête-à-tête with Jack.

As a rule, I am reluctant to get involved with a man sexually before I know him. As a rule, I break all the rules.

*!!***!!***!!*

"WHEN ARE you going to Great Expectations?" Georgina asks, determined to keep me on track.

"I'm due at the Van Buren house, the site of the engagement party. I'll go right after. I promise." I'm out of the office before she can say anything else.

Shelly Van Buren appears the way I envisioned her. She is unassuming, confident even, I surmise, by the way she greets me at the door of her Brentwood home. She moves out of the way to reveal a large living room. She leads me to the kitchen. Avocado-colored appliances with butter-yellow countertops make her look beautiful. We are nothing alike. My hair is short, short, short. I'm just a wash 'n' wear girl. I don't have time to do my hair. Hers is long, feminine, flowing natural blonde. She moves strands of hair out of her face before she extends her hand to mine. She has a well-manicured hand with long nails. My nails are short. No nail polish. Ever. Couldn't have it chipping off anywhere near a client's meal.

She looks happy. She's wearing her ring like she was born with it. I want to ask her how she did it, how they met, all the intimate girlfriend stuff I want access to impatiently. Immediately. Instead I ask if she'd mind if we use her oven the night of the party, and whether she'd like me to hire a bartender.

"No, and yes, in that order," she says.

When I mention some of my ideas for platter presentation, she brings her hand up to her mouth and squeals. "Oh, I was just expecting food. I hadn't thought about how good you could make it look."

I am motivated to find a man by her seeming success. If Shelly can do it, I can do it. I think maybe I should have been able to manage it already.

*!!***!!***!!*

It's a slow crawl over to Great Expectations. It's just east of Sepulveda Boulevard and even midafternoon, traffic is a painful trickle along Santa Monica Boulevard. At this rate I'll be watching the sun set in my rearview mirror. I have enough time to get in my own head over the task at hand. I can feel a mild anxiety building right along with my insecurity, and plain-Jane demeanor. I'm relieved to find parking right away.

Standing in the foyer of Great Expectations, I feel an air of possibility everywhere, like I'm breathing new air. Quiet expectation lines the walls with happy couple posters I can't avoid seeing. Smart-looking lights beam promise in like liquid gold. I'm doubting myself, now that I'm under these lights. I'm embarrassed and pray that I'm not humiliated by seeing someone I know. I feel like a loser to have to resort to dating this way. What am I doing here?

The last date I was on was disastrous. My friend Genevieve set me up with her friend Marco. Ages ago. He took me to a Moroccan restaurant on Westwood Boulevard and we sat on plush pillows at mosaic-topped tables. He spoke French to the waiters and was impressed when I ordered a Ricard. Big deal. I love the drink. *Merci beaucoup*. He ordered one too.

He thought dinner and a walk along the beach would earn him a sloppy kiss when we parted for the evening. Not. I just wasn't into him, and what? I have to kiss him just because he takes me to dinner? What's that all about? Had I been into him I'd have had *him* for dinner, not the Moroccan plate I'd finally settled on. I'd have been licking the Ricard off his face.

That's when I decided my menu should not include men. I decided, instead, to channel my sexuality into my work, making food my sensual reality. I would let food become my palette, and let it color me in every way. I'd thought my sexual revolution was long over. I'd even described myself as a born-again virgin, an island to be discovered in a sea of wetness. But now everything was changing. I could taste it.

A long-haired lioness of a woman greets me. She's braving a form-fitting soft blue skirt and matching blazer. She wouldn't have a problem captivating a man. I feel diminished already but try to keep my spirits up.

"Hi, Gwen, I'm Louise." She has a perfect-sounding voice.

"Hi. Thanks for helping."

"Of course. Let's start by showing you how the binders work."

She swings her arm around to reveal shelves of binders, all thick, black, and serious looking. "Men are over here. Women across the room. The profiles are updated regularly, so anyone in the binder is still looking as well. Our video library is around the corner from the binder area. You can take one binder at a time, and three videos into any of our viewing rooms. You'll see those shortly."

"Wow." There are a lot of binders. There are men and women milling about in the background.

"Yes, we're growing. We have a high success rate. Those aren't fake couples hanging on our walls. We even have video courses."

"Really?" Intrigue grips me.

"Yes. How to have the best first date, how to be the best boyfriend, or girlfriend. You know, things like that. Helpful stuff."

"That's a lot to take in at once."

The initial screening is relatively painless and is done in a private room. She makes me feel at ease until she says, "Let's start with some information about you, and your interests."

I skip over the profession part, speaking of my side interests—they don't include much other than dressing and brushing my teeth lately, but I have to come up with something. I embellish these activities convincingly. "I'm an avid reader. I like to garden. Time with friends is important."

She's jotting everything down on a long paper. "I love to garden as well. What do you like to grow?"

"Vegetables mostly."

"What do you like to read?"

"Cookbooks. I'll go to dinner parties any day of the week." I don't want every man to know I'm a chef extraordinaire or they'll be wanting me to cook for them immediately. I don't have much invested, so there's nothing to lose. I convince myself of this and try to keep an open mind.

"We'll need photographs of you. The photos help, for sure, but letting us take a video asking you questions is way better. Your personality gets to shine. Your chances of catching someone's eye go way up. It's a little more expensive, but I promise you'll feel you got your money's worth."

I opt for the video. What choice do I have?

"Heather at the front can schedule your appointment for photos and video at your convenience. Now that we've done all the paperwork, you're free to go through the binders."

I make myself comfortable in what I dub the selection chamber.

There really are binders and binders of men to choose from. I am beyond excited. Momentarily dizzied by the choice. Maybe Georgina is onto something. Young and old. Attractive. Drop-dead gorgeous, and probably too good to be true. I read, and read, flip, and flip. Like burgers on a barbecue, I inspect them like they're meat, sniffing at the seams of their personas and inconsistencies. I am suspicious—how relationship impaired are they? How emotionally defunct? What uncontrollable habits have impeded any serious relationship from blooming in their lives, let alone being sustained? I am emoting my dismay by turning some pages quickly, not allowing myself to narrow in on anyone who would probably end up disappointing me.

I know that Georgina wants results, so I jot down a few numbers and give them to Heather. She's running the desk and the matchmaker computer console on her credenza like a pro.

I return to my office, and sure enough, Georgina, already in apron and gloves, is wanting names. She's poised in the kitchen, hovering over forty chicken breasts soaking in the prep sink, softening their frozen flesh. The smell of fresh pesto is thick in the air. She has Martha tuned in.

"I can take the chicken out and put it in a pan to marinate if you want," I say above the hum of the refrigerators and freezer. I need to get my hands into something.

"Sure. If you can work and talk at the same time."

"Ha. Ha. Okay, so at the top of my list of hopefuls is Jake. He's so handsome, he seems soulful. He's a financial advisor, seems to travel a bit, so maybe we could do that together. He's got all these great pictures in beautiful outdoor vistas. He likes to mountain bike. Oh, did I mention handsome?"

"Plenty of mountains around here." Georgina backs away from the sink. "I'll get the marinade ready," she suggests.

"We're using the honey citrus sauce. One part lime to two parts lemon juice to four parts orange juice. Easy on the lemon juice if the orange juice isn't really sweet. Try it to make sure. Add honey to taste, and to thicken slightly. Pour over breasts. Marinate until the cows come home."

"You really don't have time to travel. We're booked for like ever. Who else is there?"

"There's this guy named Simon who seems as equally delicious and looks good in a suit. He likes to scuba dive but has a spark of something that's really intriguing. Very photogenic."

"How do you know? He may be so photogenic he's unattractive in person."

"Thanks for that. I'm not insecure enough, I have to second-guess my instincts?"

"You'll be fine. When do the games begin?"

"I've done my part. If they're interested, they'll call me."

I look up to see Martha on TV.

"Hey, Georgina, come see what Martha's doing. She's making Rice Krispies treats with Cap'n Crunch, Rice Krispies, and Froot Loops." Georgina is by my side instantly. "Look, she's melting the marshmallows."

"That's really good. I once put chocolate chips in mine and thought I was the cat's meow, but this, this is good," Georgina confirms.

We love Martha.

"I think I should go to the market and get some cereal. We have time to make them today. We can eat them for breakfast all day long."

"I'll buy that, Georgina, and I'm hungry."

Georgina is off before Martha mushed the cereal mixture into her baking dish on her television studio kitchen counter.

"She said six cups of cereal, but I saw her leave some behind," I report to Georgina when she comes back with the cereal boxes and bags of marshmallows.

I cross the chicken off my prep list with gusto using a neon green highlighter and reach for a handful of bamboo skewer sticks. I add water to an oblong dish and soak them. I return to my prep list and decide to tackle the platters next. I plan to place the skewered honey citrus chicken on a bed of fresh birds of paradise, the spicy Chicken Zings on a plastic-wrapped platter of small gold rings I got at the party favor store down the block. The crab salad on endive leaves will sit on a bed of fresh chopped chives tied with raffia knots.

I'm counting on Georgina to help me think of something to do with the sweet-and-sour meatballs, and the tortellini rounds, but she has offered nothing. Time is running out, but we're happily munching on neon Rice Krispies squares so our stress is barely noticeable. In fact, I take a moment to wonder whether we can even call them Rice Krispies squares anymore.

"Should we call these Frooty Cap'n Krispies? or Krispie Cap'n Frootys?"

"I don't know. I just don't know."

Georgina finishes the crab salad before bidding me a good, good night. She likes to repeat herself for effect, so she says goodbye again. I can't do anything else, so I leave my kitchen, locking up the double locks—Georgina's idea as well—and drive across town toward my happy home.

There are two-headed couples everywhere on the streets, and in the cars passing me. They can't all be together, I tell myself. Some of them are undoubtedly brothers and sisters—platonic friends even. I can't be the only single one left out of the pairing pairs, can I? I am aware of a silent longing I've not allowed myself to feel and am lonely. Alone. I am a singular, not a plural. I am longing for any of the binder boys waiting for me in the selection chamber as I fall asleep.

Later Georgina calls me with her ideas. "Let's cut out banana leaf hearts. Oversized ones. And put them on the platter under the tortellini rounds. The pasta's multicolored and will look great against the dark green leaves."

"I like it," I admit sleepily.

"And little radish roses to offset the meatballs."

"You're getting good at this," I say and wish her good night.

"Night, night."

*!!***!!***!!*

I DO spend a lot of time in the kitchen. I rarely get out of it at all except to shop and sleep. It's not surprising that I haven't been able to manage a relationship thus far. I've practically given up anyway after such bumbled attempts. I have the recipe for doomed singledom apparently.

In the past, I preferred the conquest of an irresistible man to the idea that the connection might linger. I wasn't interested in attachments. Perhaps a manly approach to think of someone as a conquest, but it was undeniably true. I can't get beyond the fantasy. I don't need to know all the savory details of a man's life. Sex is story enough.

I rush into sex because I want to get the best out of a man before he disappoints me, before I see flaws in him I can't accept for the duration. Now, however, is not the time to sacrifice the long term for instant gratification. I have to admit my longing to try. Whether I feel I can do it at all seems not to be the point, rather that I should at least be willing to try. I need to be my own friend here and look carefully before I leap into the arms of another penis-bearing person. Despite this challenge, I am motivated, and reinvigorated.

Morning comes as a welcome gift, and I am in my kitchen before I know I'm even out of bed.

Georgina probes, "Okay, what's his name?"

"Whose name?" I ask, caught up in the portioning of chicken for Shelly and Adam's fast approaching engagement party.

"The guy."

I'm catching on. I'm also feeling feisty so I'm going to make her work for this.

"What guy?"

"Oh, don't be ridiculous. *'What guy?'*" she says, mocking me like I'm an idiot. "I know there's some shining star stud at the top of the list already."

"Oh, don't be ridiculous," I say, mocking her, "your expectations are too high already. It's too soon to say. They're all just first names and posed photographs. Who can tell?"

"You can tell a lot from a photograph."

"And I can tell by looking at the clock we're going to have to get a move on." If I could play this hard to get with men I'd probably be married already. "The oven's on. I have to bake the meatballs."

"You bake your meatballs?"

"Well, somebody's got to."

"My mother always boiled hers in sauce," she says, like she's been misled.

"That works, too, but it's a bit messy for skewers. I bake mine dry, then sauce them up later."

*!!***!!***!!*

THERE COMES a time before every party that I realize I'm as ready as I'll ever be, and whatever fussing and mussing left to do transfers from my kitchen to the location via the Lip-Mobile. We are in the back of it making sure everything is just right before we leave. There is shelving that makes it easy to store our nonperishables, and the accoutrements we take from job to job. Georgina and I custom-painted it after Philip sanded it for us. He did an amazing job because the paint went on like butter.

We used mayonnaise white as a base—it wasn't really called that, but that's what it looked like to me—it had some depth to it. Georgina took it to the next level with black trim around the exterior lights and doors. A week later we stamped giant lip outlines and painted those in with shades of red. It's flashy and elegant.

We are organized enough to have not forgotten anything vital for the Van Buren affair.

She's passing the crab salad, sauces, and the giant tortellini rounds to me, all packed in stackable clear boxes with lids, and I'm loading them into our onboard refrigerator when I tell her, "I want to stay in the kitchen this time, and just make the food look pretty. I don't want to go out there and pass hors d'oeuvres."

Her shock shows. Her eyebrows tell me she can't believe I'd pass up the opportunity to mingle. "What? But it's so you to be out there talking to the eating public. I mean, you're Lip Service. It's you."

*Yeah, I did enough mingling at the Mother's Day brunch*, I think. She probably thinks so, too, but she's not saying. *Or is she?*

*!!***!!***!!*

THERE IS a swing door between the kitchen and living room at the Van Buren residence. Party noise filters in and out while I work, gathering momentum as the wine bottles empty. There are people everywhere. I try not to look into the crowd. There's bound to be one man out there I might consider worthy of torrid behavior.

Shelly Van Buren comes into the kitchen. The ceramic tile-topped countertop looks like it was installed recently in a purposely retro way. It's hip, and chic. It makes Shelly look like one groovy chick. She watches while I skewer the chicken, the tender strips still plump and warm from the oven. I am chewing on a Chicken Zing discreetly. I don't like my clients to know I eat. At least not at their expense. She looks at the chicken like it is beyond her while I swallow quietly. She leans into the counter. I think she's had a few toasts too many.

"I don't know how you did this," she says to me, amazed, trying to stand straight. And then, "Adam's buying me a convection oven as soon as we're married. I don't know what he's thinking. I think he's more traditional than I'd imagined. I just don't have the heart to tell him it's not going to make any difference."

I let her talk while I platter the chicken, ready for Georgina and her next pass. It's like a relay race, and the guests are a hungry, toasting crowd. Georgina and I say nothing to each other. We prefer a code of silence whenever possible. We like to concentrate, and we believe the food should speak for itself. A smile passes between Georgina and Shelly as I pass the tray to Georgina. Shelly's smile is trepidatious, brimming with uncertainty. Georgina's smile shines with comforting competence. She seems instantly to calm Shelly. I love that about Georgina. She makes her way into the living room with another tray.

A more confident version of Shelly is left behind. Adam Gaines, the-stubble-on-his-chin-manly-man, enters as though he's been looking for her. Her soon-to-be husband gushes at her side, and grabs a Chicken Zing, content to know his soon-to-be wife is safe here in the kitchen. He kisses her on the cheek and leaves as quickly as he came.

"What am I going to do?" she whimpers. "I don't even own a pair of oven mitts."

"Tell him every oven should come with a pair," I suggest.

While our expertise may have done nothing but shine a disturbing light on Shelly's culinary inadequacies, she still thanks us profusely for our services, and rewards us with a healthy tip at the end of the evening. She presses it into the pocket of my apron, blushing as she withdraws her hand.

"Thank you so much. I already know some of my friends are going to call you."

*!!***!!***!!*

"WHEN, GWEN? Men, Gwen?" I ask, pinching my cheeks, watching them turn red through the reflection in my bathroom mirror. I know I'll have to give them time to get back to me, all those hopeful romantic types I chose the other day.

I think of Shelly. I want what she's got. I wonder how many men she climbed through to snap her man. She seemed so happy, so sure of herself, until she admitted she couldn't cook. She's inspired me so much I vow to give her cooking lessons. A small repertoire of no-fail recipes, and the assurance that she, too, can cook. "Yes, yes, you, too, can cook," I'll say, full of zeal. There is much to do, but I am tired.

Fallen onto my bed, my hands are sleepily massaging the side of my neck, silently tracing the line of my collar bone. Moving to my waist, my hand grabs at the silky flesh at my side, hip bone protruding. I am aroused suddenly by my own softness and the possibility of a loving man loving me, and the feeling of his five o'clock shadow against my skin.

Down my hips, along my outer thigh, daringly to my inner thigh and up into my private haven, my pleasure center. I wonder if I have the energy to please myself now after working all night. It feels good to be touched even by my own hands. I let them have their way with me until my body shudders with orgasm and I fall asleep feeling hopeful.

# Chapter Three

## Richmond Surprise Birthday Party

Sit-Down Menu for 12
Mixed Field Greens with Raspberry Tarragon Vinaigrette
Rosemary Risotto with Smoked Chicken Cubes
Garlic & Ginger Crusted Fillet of Salmon
Roasted Tomato Discs with Basil & Oregano
Glazed Carrots & Asparagus Spears
Chocolate Decadence

I'm in trouble. I'm in overwhelm. They've all started calling back. I'm wanted in two counties. I can't keep them straight. Jonathan. Dan. Simon. Jake. Joel. Peter. With so many to choose from, I'll have to be picky, picky, picky. As picky as I am about my produce. Only the best for me. As for the ones who have picked me, they could be hoping I'll be their next great love or token luster, right now. The landscape of my week stretches before me. I'd said yes to all of them thinking it wasn't fair to not give them that telling first date. Why not meet them all? Who am I to stand in love's way? I'm like a kid in a candy store, eyes wide, unbelieving, mouth drooling.

Thankfully I've hammered out the most important details with Sophia Richmond, so her party is on track. I've worked on it intermittently for days already. Good thing, I'll be busy sifting through men—all these hopefuls—to get to the one true love I'm searching for.

Great Expectations sends me a list of guys interested in me, which adds to my list of potentials. I dial them one by one from my office. I realize one of the guys who picked me is an exterminator. I pause to ponder. I know, it's good to keep an open mind, but I need to get real. I just don't see myself with a man who owns a pest-control company. An average conversation might be: "Hi, honey, what did you kill today?" I mean what kind of pet name do you give to such a man. Killer? I can't do a first date. I just can't, and in a few days, reason will temper my guilt.

When Joel, one of my picks, says he's hung around his apartment all day watching Saturday morning cartoons and playing with Power Rangers, I immediately lose all interest in him. I can't do a primary date with him either. He probably eats Cocoa Puffs during commercial breaks. And no, I can't come out to play. It doesn't matter that I eat tooti-frooti neon Rice Krispies squares either. I look at my watch, and wince. I've already given Joel twenty minutes of my time. Despite my fears of becoming a cereal monogamist, I wind up the call, deciding I'd be better off making tomato discs and roasting them. I put my list away and join Georgina in the kitchen. She's already chopped the thick ends off the asparagus and has moved on to peeling the spears with a vegetable peeler.

Georgina is in a chatty mood and wants to talk about her boyfriend, Philip. The one she's just moved in with after months and months of badgering him to let her. She's sooo in love, she says, over and over, and wants to marry him. Something about their relationship sounds fishy to me. She never talks about their sex life. Like maybe it's not important.

"When I think about marrying a man, I don't think about whether I want to be with him all my life, I think about whether I want to be with his penis for the rest of my life," I say. I don't entirely mean it. I'm more into the shock value of my statement.

Georgina's mouth drops open.

"I doubt I'll be marrying a man who is not well endowed in the lower regions," I say. "It would never last. I have a serious amount of penis envy to contend with. I need him to have something I can envy."

She stops what she's doing with the asparagus.

"Don't look at me like that. I'm serious. All right, I know to a certain extent it's not the meat, it's the motion, and all that, but I need to be honest with myself. I'm going to start looking elsewhere if my man's thing-thing isn't doing the thing for me."

"But it's about love. How can you minimize it by—"

"My whole point is that I can't minimize it." Her knowledge of the elements of a marriage are lost on me. For the moment. I am off on my own tangent. "Don't you get it? I would be dreadfully miserable with a small penis. I'd simply have to have an affair. I know I'd be kidding myself to think otherwise."

The phone rings. I am expecting a call from Sophia Richmond, my birthday party client. I've had her file open on my desk. Georgina's mouth is still open, but she resumes her work with the asparagus. Sophia needs to make adjustments to our plans, so I take notes, and then finish our phone call.

"All right, I need to think for a minute. The birthday menu. The surprise party thing. There's a schedule change. I'm going to send you early with the appetizers. Sophia can get her husband, Clarence, out of the house, but he's coming back too soon. We'll figure it out." I make the notes and close her file.

I want to pick up where we left off. "Okay. Back to this penis thing. Don't tell me you don't care what size a penis is?" I ask incredulously. I am already in shock before her reply.

"I've never really thought about it."

Now *my* mouth was hanging open.

"How can you not think about it? Okay, okay, wait. You might not think about it, but how could you miss feeling it?" A thought strikes me suddenly. My hand is at my forehead shielding my eyes. Could it be true?

Georgina is disturbed by my prying, but I cannot stop. "Oh, my god, don't tell me." I look at her as though for the first time. "Don't tell me you don't touch it. Are you one of those? Is that it? Honey, who raised you? I mean did your parents have sex, did they skip over all that, or what?"

She could not have been quieter, standing against the butcher block, cleavers within easy reach.

"Look, I'm trying to save your marriage here," I vow.

"But I'm not married yet." Her redheaded, freckled-face demeanor becomes confused, her mouth pouty.

"You may never be unless you take my advice. Look how long it took for you to move in together. The man had his reservations already. You had to talk him into it. You'd best find a way to get in the mood, because that boy's not marrying someone who isn't putting out enough *before* the wedding, I assure you. So, whatever you need to do to get into the mood for oral sex, get on with it."

"But I can't—"

"What? You want all the attention for yourself? Is that it? Don't be so selfish. I just don't understand women who don't like sex. It's beyond my realm of comprehension. Sex is not just about you in case you haven't figured that out yet."

Georgina works faster when she's annoyed, so our menu prep is done in record time. I spend a few more minutes on my list of hopefuls before I call it a day.

*!!***!!***!!*

My first date is with Jonathan. Six two. Magazine salesman. Catholic by birth. He says on his video he is new to LA and is trying to meet people. Smart approach, I think, and hey, why not say yes to his request for a date—maybe I can show him around LA. Little miss helpful.

Well, I come to find out his video was done five years ago. So not only does he not need me to help him find anything in this vast city, but he's lost the cute baby face he had in the video. He warns me about this, but swears he's still cute. I add five years to the mental picture I have of him and decide *what the heck.*

I am running about five minutes late for our date already, and another few minutes behind because parking on Main Street in Venice is time consuming and I haven't planned for it. I see Jonathan hunched in the doorway of a shoe store as I drive by. I know it's him. I've seen his picture. He is dressed like a square. I honk, hoping he'll notice me and see that I haven't stood him up.

I wave, *it's me, Gwen, the binder girl. The girl you're having dinner with, the girl who's late for our first date. The girl who—.* He manages a small wave in my direction, although he is obviously distracted. A homeless woman is standing beside him in the doorway, talking to him, moving closer, almost backing him into the doorframe. I watch him reach into his pocket. A few bills come out, and he hands them to her. She takes the money from him with her left hand, shoos him away with her right. Through my rearview mirror, I can see him coming out of the doorway. He shrugs her off, stands more boldly in the middle of the sidewalk. He's seen my photographs and video. I am sure he recognizes me. *I am the binder girl.* I park at the Coffee Bean and hope I don't get towed.

The patio tables are nearly all filled in. He tells the hostess he'd prefer to sit inside. At the same time, he turns around to me and says, "Is this okay? We could go somewhere else."

"It's fine," I say. The hostess leads us into the restaurant. He turns around again.

"Are you sure this is okay? Or would you prefer to go somewhere else?"

By now I'm thinking, *hey, we're here, let's eat. I'm hungry.*

"This place is noisy. I'm not great with noise," he admits loudly, so he can be heard. I can tell he doesn't like to raise his voice.

I'd already taken my seat. A menu is thrust into my hand by the hostess. It might be too late to go anywhere. He's standing, his hand on his chair, reluctant to sit, looking around over his shoulder as if that might alter the noise level in the room. There are trendy avant-gardes all over the place. He looks a little lost,

Mr. Tall in his plaid shirt. He resigns himself to the situation—hey, it was his idea to come here—and sits down. He is momentarily preoccupied with the other women coming and going through the restaurant.

He shrinks in his seat, slumped, defeated. He continues to look over his shoulder, to the right, to the left, as he asks me questions. The usual ream of inquiries without really paying attention to me in my braless outfit. How long have you lived here, what are your goals, short term, long term, blah blah blah. I feel like he's trying to meet some sales quota of inquiries. He laughs at me when I tell him I don't own jeans and haven't been out on a date in more than two years. Like I'm lying. He checks his watch frequently, casually, as if I don't notice. Maybe he's on a deadline, or maybe he's timing himself, trying to see how long he can stand the noise in this out-of-his-element kind of place.

Okay, so it isn't a good match here, he and I—the we, we would never be—but we are sharing the intimate act of dining nonetheless. Grilled vegetables over couscous, and spinach cakes for me, spaghetti carbonara for him. He becomes sullen and preoccupied, so I study the grill marks on my vegetables, and the way the zucchini has been arranged on my plate.

I would never have thought of adding beets to the couscous, I'd have worried the beets would stain the grain, and I knew suddenly why events had transpired the way they had. What a breakthrough. The tinted couscous was festive, soulful—flashy, even. I had more compassion for Jonathan immediately.

I was already thinking about a Christmas couscous. He might not fill the role of boyfriend, possible husband, but he was an ambassador of the restaurant world, and its cornucopia of food fancy.

He has inadvertently led me to a culinary epiphany, so when he asks if I'd like to see him again, I have to say, "Yes."

"A quieter restaurant next time."

"Okay. I'd like that." He has no idea.

I vow to try that thing with the couscous at my first opportunity, and I decide I would sleep with him. But not tonight. I'd save him for a rainy day.

*!!***!!***!!*

When Jake calls the next day, I am already up to my elbows in ideas for Shelly Van Buren's bridal shower. Hearts, hearts, hearts. Tarts, tarts, tarts. Tarts for two, two for tarts, but enough of them to feed pounds of people. The sound of his voice pulls my concentration right off base. I'm thinking first base, second base. Finally. I'd been hoping he'd call.

Pleasantries out of the way, he asks to meet me for lunch. Tomorrow. He's anxious but he's playing it safe. I sense he is cautious. It strikes me that a lunch date over a dinner date might be a preference for many men. Lunch is more like a meeting than a date. It is safer. It's easier to meet at the restaurant. A dinner date might imply the girl has to be picked up. Afternoons are less threatening, and if he doesn't like her, she can buy her own lunch. To be safe, I won't be going to lunch hungry.

I knew I'd be able to see him, still have enough time to put the finishing touches on Sophia's dinner party and make it to their house in time to set up and *Surprise!!* husband Clarence. We agree on time and place. I like the sound of his voice more the longer he talks, and when we hang up, I jump from my desk forgetting Shelly's menu altogether.

I grab the sweater from the back of my chair. I need to see what he looks like. "I'm going to the selection chamber," I tell Georgina and scurry out the door.

"And I'm going to the walk-in refrigerator," she says with an edge in her voice.

I don't have any conscious recollection of driving to the Great Expectations offices, but my car is parked in front of the building. I was in my head the whole way over. I was thinking about love. True love. Heart-pounding love. I'd kept myself from thinking I could have it, but I want it. I want to be loved, adored, revered. Caressed, and otherwise fondled too. I match his number and name to the binder I would find him in and pull his video.

Oh, he's the financial advisor, I realize when I looked at his profile, but he doesn't look conservative despite his square jaw. He's the rugged type. Loves the great outdoors—hiking, mountain biking. His picture in the binder shows a healthy rugged complexion. Nice smile lines in the corners of his eyes. He's taller than I am and has a lean, athletic frame. I dismiss the typos in his profile because it reads easily, nonetheless, and it says he's looking for the love of his life, the woman he can share his life with. A mutual mutuality and all that. Maybe we are onto something.

When I get back to the kitchen, Georgina emerges from the walk-in with ginger and cloves of garlic. "You haven't been in there this whole time, have you?" I mock.

She answers with a "ha!" then ignores me.

Knowing I like to marinate my salmon for a day prior to searing it, she sets about the task of mincing both the garlic and ginger until there are heaps of it to rub over the salmon.

"Hey, don't forget to sprinkle both sides of the salmon with ground cumin, coriander, and black pepper before the garlic and ginger mixture goes on."

"Yeah, yeah, I'll sprinkle it."

She is lippy today.

*!!***!!***!!*

I SEAR the salmon as soon as I get to the kitchen the next morning and have Georgina pull the smoker for the chicken we would be adding to the risotto. The kitchen is filled with thick aromas in no time. I have three hours until "d" date. I am not going to be late. Not today.

"Let's get the water boiling for the carrots. Blanch the asparagus. Tray a small piece of the salmon for us—wrap the rest and get it back into the fridge—we'll finish baking it at Sophia's. The raspberries need to be puréed then pressed through cheesecloth before we make the vinaigrette." I go on and on giving Georgina instructions, not that she couldn't read them right off our master list, taped to the refrigerator. I am so nervous my lips just keep moving.

"That's a lot of lip service, Gwen. Thanks for saving me the walk over there to see for myself though."

I like that Georgina has no trouble with multitasking. She's a powerhouse. At noon, we break to eat a small sampling of Sophia's menu. The rosemary risotto is so creamy. I remember I have to pick up the cake at Sweet Temptations. With a quick look at my watch, I calculate how much time I can spend on my lunch date and am gone.

I want the rip the donut hole center out of the donut and eat it kind of love that fills me up with the bittersweet gift of life. I realize this as I sit across from Jake. I am tempted by his eyes and the fine line of his jaw, his eyes the color of honey. I want to swim in that gooey honey place and spread my arms apart in a glorious salute to love. Swim and slither, suspended in the sticky weightlessness of it all. I am watching him—the way the fork enters his mouth, first over his lips, a flash of tongue as he tastes it. Seeing him now I want to fall and fall, and fall. I notice how strong his jaw is, appreciate his strength of body. He can't catch all the linguine heading for his mouth, strands spill out and fall back to his plate, eluding his bite. *Oh.*

Things aren't so dreamy suddenly. *I could never be with a man who eats linguine like this*, I insist to myself, indignant. *He isn't even aware of the way he's chewing—sucking it up into his mouth like it were meaningless, letting it fall back to his plate without recourse.*

I debate silently over whether I want to go through the motions of getting to know him. I know looking at him, it isn't going to work. I'd let my guard down, he'd impress me for about as long as it would take to bake my creole chicken—which I decided I wouldn't be baking for him—and then it'd be done. The dishes would be cleared, the meal would be over.

I could never be with a man who eats linguine like this. I knew he'd make love to me that way. Sloppily. He'd probably have a problem with premature ejaculation, or never take the time to discover that I'm orgasmic multiplied. My heart is heavy with this realization. I can feel it in my stomach along with the lunch I'd already eaten. It weighs against me. Sadness. I breathe it in and out, exhaling heavily, trying to let it pass.

I didn't even notice I'd stopped eating. I pray silently to the food gods as I watch him lift his fork to his mouth again and chew. My heart is in my tongue as I silently mouth the words. Hear my prayer: *Food Gods, don't let him start talking with his mouth full. I'll make a scene and run right out of here and he'll have to pay for lunch. Oh, good God.*

When we finish lunch, the waiter clears our plates to reveal several strands of linguine stuck against the tablecloth, some of it all the way over near my plate.

I am intent on getting away from him, he is intent on following. I let him walk me to my car and bid him goodbye. Huh! I wouldn't bet my next meal on it.

I pick up Clarence Richmond's birthday cake on my way back to my kitchen—a place I can't wait to get to. My head fills with visions of a man I do not know. He respects food and chews properly. He's that and so much more. Ugh. I want to share my life. I do, I realize. I'll do what I can to let go of my defenses, to not let my cynicism rule. My prayer continues. *Please Gods and Goddesses, give me more to work with.*

*!!***!!***!!*

THE RICHMOND home in the Palisades is like a scenic stop at the side of a road that affords breathtaking views of the surrounding landscape. Many of the walls are glass with stained-glass insets that allow a view of the Pacific Ocean and bordering mountains. At night the lights of Malibu glitter in the distance like an open jewelry box.

Georgina already has the workstation in the kitchen set up and has determined how Sophia wants the table set by the time I arrive. She is busy setting the ambience.

"It didn't go well," she says. She already knows. We're alone in the kitchen.

"Don't ask," I plead. I don't want to have to explain my point of reasoning for not giving Jake another chance. "And don't make faces." I can't handle any of her looks right now. I check my watch. Clarence is due within the hour.

Sophia enters the kitchen to say hello. She is kind and speaks softly. She is vibrant, and enthusiastic about the party she's throwing her husband. She's wearing a dress that drapes to the floor. She is pleased so far with our work and confident we'll do a great job. Her bracelet catches in the light and she looks elegant, sophisticated.

We hear the doorbell then and move a little faster. Sophia remains calm and poised. She smiles widely, puts her glass down on the countertop, and makes her way to the front door. We preheat the oven for the salmon, assemble the salads individually on plates we've already chilled, and make room for the cake in the fridge. Decadent, indeed. I find matches and light the candles on the dining table. We can hear Sophia greeting guests at the front door. I put the appetizers into the oven while Georgina opens the wine. I taste the risotto Georgina is commandeering at the stove. It is perfect. We're ready.

The guests are a faceless ensemble of characters. They are regal and their excitement builds as the time comes for Clarence to return from golfing. One of them likes the appetizers and asks for recipes. I can't admit I haven't made them myself, so I flub my way through how I would do them if I had made them. One rule in catering is that it's made from scratch even if it isn't. Never admit you didn't make it yourself. One of the men spots Clarence's car coming up the driveway.

"Everyone! He's here."

Some grab for their wine glasses, some pop another appetizer in their mouth. They all congregate at the front door. Sophia is radiantly expectant and all is a hush. The door opens. "*Surprise! Surprise!*" we hear in syncopated beats from the kitchen. Clarence clutches his heart in a mock heart attack. Glasses clink and everyone laughs.

The dining table is surrounded by three walls of glass, and as the sun sets, it illuminates the room. When darkness falls, the ocean blackens. The room becomes a shimmering, glowing atmosphere as the stained glass reflects the flame from candles and the shining coastline. The whole room dances with light. The setting is surreal and magical.

I sneak glimpses of Sophia and Clarence throughout the night, in between the courses we serve leisurely. I plate the food and Georgina passes it. I am in awe of Sophia. I watch from the archway between kitchen and dining room. So clearly is she in love with her husband and he with her. They've been together for thirty years, I learn through one of the female guests, who leaves the table and comes into the kitchen to smoke a cigarette between courses. She's got the back door open and is blowing smoke outside, emitting details of Sophia and Clarence's life together. She envies them their relationship. I do too. How'd they do it? I can't even get a guy who eats his linguine properly. I watch them for the rest of the night, hoping I'll learn something. The party is a great success, but I go home hungry.

*!!***!!***!!*

THIS WHOLE dating thing is depressing, too, I decide, now that I'm safe at home. Here I thought I'd have a good chance at meeting someone I could really connect to and now I doubt it all. I just want to go to sleep. The whole thing makes me want to eat gummy bears. I go into the kitchen and grab a handful out of the clear jar I keep them in for emergencies. There are other jars for other emergencies, but the gummy bears are the most important now.

I stuff a few into my mouth and look at the ones remaining in my hand. As soon as I swallow the ones I'm chewing, I'll eat them, too, but first I just look at them. I take one out of the palm of my hand and place it in front of another. Standing up and facing each other. They are both that yellow translucent neon gummy bear color. I press their faces together in a sticky kiss embrace and think to myself, *Yeah that's it, that's what I'm looking for.* Connection. Sticky and sweet and entirely edible.

Knowing what I know, I get depressed again and pop those bears into my mouth and chew. Honestly, I don't feel any better. Have I lost my window of opportunity?

*!!***!!***!!*

I'M GLUED to the chair in my office, working on the menu for Shelly Van Buren's bridal shower now that I've got her proposal nailed down, when the deliveryman arrives. I had been checking my watch intermittently, shuffling through paperwork at my desk waiting for him. Now that he's here, I'm shamelessly watching, out of the corner of my eye, as he approaches the back door. I can see him through the steel gate that seals me in for the day. I'm back to my wanton ways. He's got a dolly stacked with boxes. Red peppers and onions and spinach and the pine nuts I've ordered in bulk.

I can practically see his muscles flexing as he pushes the load up over the doorframe and into my domain. He's new, or maybe just a replacement for the day. I have a thing for him already.

Usually I let Georgina check the delivery inventory list, but I am drawn like metal to a magnet and have that slip of paper in my hand before the Pillsbury dough boy can say *he he he.*

I'm inspecting the fresh peppers and the hot house tomatoes as Georgina mocks me behind the deliveryman's back. Again, with the looks.

I want to place another order immediately, hoping he'll come back. I'm already wondering what I may have forgotten.

"The chicken. I forgot to order the fresh chicken breasts I need." Actually, I didn't forget at all—I'd planned to get them directly from my meat purveyor.

The name tag on his shirt lapel reads Fernando. There was no plan but Fernando. *I'll bet he knows how to eat his linguine.* I flatter myself by thinking he's as captivated by me as I am with him.

I tell him I want him to bring me my chicken. "How soon can you get it? How soon can you bring it?"

"I'll see what I can do."

I wipe imaginary sweat off my brow and mouth *thank you* without saying it out loud, lest Georgina get involved. I hand him his copy of the delivery slip. I wish I'd given Georgina the day off and could entice him into staying for lunch. He could be my plat du jour any day.

My fantasy ends as I watch him wheel his dolly over the threshold of my metal door. He is gone, but he'll be back. We speculate on his abilities as a lover and explore all possibilities. Georgina doesn't want to participate but she knows I need *someone* to talk to. "It's better you concentrate on the work of finding a husband, I think," she says.

I'm watching Fernando get away. I'll never snag a husband if I keep pursuing sexual liaisons with strangers. She agrees to that.

"Oh, well," I say, "it's better that I'm left to my own devices."

She gives me a look that wants further elaboration but is afraid to ask.

"Define devices," she says, just to make sure.

"You know. Things that go whirl in the night."

"A vibrator," she says, like she's burped it up and is diminished.

"Of course."

"I didn't know you had one."

"It was a gift."

"Really? From whom?"

"From Tim. When we were breaking up. He showed up with it one night and told me goodbye. Wished me luck. Handed me the box. I was stunned I must admit. But I'm happy now."

"No doubt. Well, I'm going to wish you luck with the rest of your day. I'll see you tomorrow."

Fernando returns with the chicken several hours later. My mind was on tarts. Warm tarts, cold tarts, sweet and savory tarts. Onion tarts, tomato and cheese tarts, spinach tarts, and even fruit tarts. I had forgotten him, entirely. I reach for the small box of chicken and put it in the fridge.

"May I use your bathroom?" he asks, heavily accented.

"Sure, it's through that door," I reply, pointing.

"Can I have a glass of water?" he asks when he returns from the bathroom.

"Sure, use the dispenser water over there. The cups are there too," I reply, pointing again. I am amused. Captivated. I watch him move. He's sure of himself. He moves like he has all the time in the world. He fills the cup with water and comes back to me. Stands really close. I've forgotten the tarts. Entirely.

"It's hot in here," he says, and unbuttons the two top buttons on his shirt.

"Sure is," I reply, smirking.

"This is the first break I've had all day," he says, and leans against my butcher block, puts the cup of water down, folds his arms across his chest, and fixes his gaze upon me, devouring me with his eyes.

I am watching his every move. I can see where this is going. I am motionless like the cheese before a mouse strikes. The mouse before the cat strikes. The deer before the headlights hit. The mouth before the lips kiss. He has me up on that butcher block and splayed like a slab of meat before I know what hits me.

# Chapter Four

## Van Buren Tarts with Heart Bridal Shower

Hot & Cold Buffet Menu for 30

Roasted Red Pepper & Tarragon Chicken Pasta Salad in Phyllo Nests

Three Onion Tart

Tomato Gruyère Tart with Basil Confetti

Spinach Tarts with Pine Nut Crust

Crème Patisserie Fruit Tarts

Chocolate Rings

First impressions are lasting ones, and that's just not fair in the dating game. I already feel at a disadvantage. Not every date is a great one, nor is every situation going to bring out the best in me. I'm uncertain in my ability to attract someone for any longer than a few clandestine meetings. I know I'm flawed—why else would I be hiding in my kitchen—but let's give love a chance anyway.

I'm hoping any of these guys will give me two, even three dates before he shrugs me off into the no-go pile of rejects, even if I never wanted to give guys a second chance. I'd already passed judgment on Jake so now I was damning my own ruthlessness. What if I don't like him and he wants to drop me at the door and then come in?

I don't want just anyone to know where I live, whether it's a good date or not. And if I don't like him, I might have to fend off his kisses at my door. There is tit for tat in the dating game, I'm sure, and somehow rebuking Jake might come back to haunt me. As for the ones I may end up liking, so much could go wrong.

Primary, secondary, third date—all have their own expectations. Heaven help me if I like one of them. I wouldn't want to be missing any kissing at my front door. I doubt I'd be able to stop myself. I'd have him inside faster than you can say *hold the mayo*. Get beyond that and then there's the pacing of a potential relationship. One wrong move and it could all be over.

And what to wear? I have so much to contend with. Clothes are especially difficult to choose for dates. What I might wear out to lunch alone is drastically different from what I might choose for a lunch date with a sailor. This is my challenge today. Lunch with Dan the sailor man.

If Dan ended up being the man, it probably wouldn't matter what I wore. I couldn't let this attitude stop me from trying to dress the part. I don't own any blue and white gingham or any nifty T-shirts with anchor emblems sewn into them, or even deck shoes for that matter, so already I was feeling like I might have missed the boat on this one. But then again, maybe I'd be just what he'd been looking for. His very own catch of the day.

Of all places to meet. Shabu Shabu for Japanese. His suggestion. Sounds okay if you're good with chopsticks. I am not especially adept at using them. I am really good, however, with my Henkel knives. I really wish I had one now. I'd use it to cut away my self-consciousness and expose my confidence. I am so nervous about this chopstick thing it takes me a while to notice that Dan is shy.

It's difficult to have lunch with a shy man. He's hearty at least. I notice while he uses his chopsticks—he's an old pro—that his hands have premature age spots from all the sailing sun. His eyes are the color of the sea and he speaks quietly, eloquently even, about the nautical miles he's covered in the last several years.

"I've been in and out of every inlet this side of the Pacific. Up north, down south. I've been so far east it's turned to west."

"Do you have favorite places?" I ask, still tortured with the chopsticks. I'm aiming for a piece of broccoli crown, hoping, praying I can get it. I'm worried, though, practically petrified. I am sure I'm burning more calories just trying to eat lunch than any I might actually ingest at this meal. I may go home hungry no matter how much I eat.

"I love the Caribbean. The sun, the clouds, the aqua water, the heat," he says.

I watch him, as he fishes through the food on his plate looking for something. He sees what he's searching for and moves in. In nanoseconds he's captured the smallest piece of beef in his chopsticks and is successfully raising it to his mouth, a prisoner, banished to the secret life of his stomach. My mouth is hanging open. He's so sexy. So mature. So capable. I am lured by his hearty personality.

"I'm really just looking for someone I can sail around the world with. It gets lonely out there at sea."

Now I *know* I'll be going home hungry. Hungry for another chance. I strike him off my list. *Next!* Too bad, sexy. I like the earth beneath my feet. I can't set sail for a new world. I have a bridal shower to cater. My clients would be so disappointed. I relax instantly. I am able, suddenly, and much to my surprise and instant joy, to bring the broccoli crown into safe waters in my own mouth.

"Well, thanks for lunch, Dan," I say when we're outside. "It was really nice meeting you."

"Can I tempt you with a little dessert?" he asks, his hand on my elbow. "I don't live far from here."

"Oh, perhaps another time. I really have to run." *Literally. If I don't run away now, I won't stand a chance.*

I'd be better off slicing my onions for my three-onion tart than wondering what to make of Dan right now. I make a mental list of what still needs to be done for Shelly's event while I drive back to my kitchen. There are bunches of spinach to sauté and vine-ripened tomatoes to slice. I caramelize the onions for the onion tart and try to keep their rings intact. After giving Georgina her prep list for the afternoon, I give her an update on my list of hopefuls and think out loud while I clean the spinach.

"I think this is hopeless," I say without further elaboration.

"What, the spinach?"

"No. This whole dating game thing." I'm working on a few theories and am not ready to share them with Georgina. "Although, it probably wouldn't hurt to have our vendor bring in cleaned spinach next time."

One. If I date men I am not attracted to, I could stave off a sudden case of the must-have-sex syndrome. This, however, would only work if I'd had sex recently with someone I'm attracted to. Having not had sex recently would make an undesirable man irresistible under the right—making them the wrong—circumstances and blowing my theory altogether. Oh, for the power of come. I am lost without it. I'm still amazed I didn't let Dan take me out to the harbor.

Allison, Shelly's soon to be sister-in-law, is hosting the bridal shower and is eager to do a walk-through of her home to determine how best to decorate and where our buffet will be served. I promised to be there by three P.M. Her directions were perfect. I'd never been up in that corner of LA horse country before. Rolling hills and ranch-style fencing stretched for miles. She opens the front door before I'm even halfway up her front path.

"Oh, good. You're right on time. That makes me feel confident you'll do a good job."

She gives me the tour with a no-nonsense approach.

"Given the higher temperatures, I'd prefer to use the patio as the backdrop for the festivities."

Given the full sun beating down on the patio now at three in the afternoon, I worry about the integrity of our precious tarts and how they will fare with all that radiance.

"Let's consider a tent to shield the two food stations, and umbrellas over the tables."

"Good idea. Do they come in green?" I nodded. "Now, Shelly is to know nothing about this," Allison says. "I'll be so disappointed if she found out. Her mom is taking her to lunch after the final fitting for her wedding dress and dropping her here to discuss flower arrangements for the wedding. Or so she thinks. Of course, we'll all be waiting, and you'll have everything you need, and we'll all have a grand time."

I get back to the office to find messages from both Jonathan and Dan wanting follow-up dates. Dan is suggesting an outdoor concert at the Santa Monica Pier and a sunset sail. Jonathan has a museum outing in mind. I suspect they have both been saving up ideas for outings and are now hoping to exercise them with the girl of their choice. Jake calls while I am forming tart shells. I'm not anxious to see him after the linguine incident so I tell him I am sooo busy with the bridal shower that I won't be available for more than a week.

I am willing, however, to meet with Peter. I hadn't met him yet and his profile intrigues me. I was hoping our lifestyles were better matched than Dan's and mine. I think I might be able to fit in a cup of coffee one afternoon this week. We agree to meet at Urth Caffé.

He's waiting for me at a table in the corner. I come in carrying things I'd picked up at the party store around the corner and put them on the floor beside me. He nervously drags his hand across his hair and then extends it to me in hello. I notice his creative part immediately. He has the nervous habit of smoothing his hair over his bald spot when talking about himself, so if I hadn't caught it right away, I surely would have by then.

My age is showing in unexpected ways. Six years ago, Peter's part would have been more normal. Men have less and less hair now in my world. I find a fully bald man sexy and appealing. A fully haired scalp with a proper hairline is equally appealing—all these in-between stages are a turnoff and make me feel old. I wonder if Peter thinks I can't see the bald patch under the pieces of hair he's got combed clear across his head.

*!!***!!***!!*

If a man had any idea what effect fine dining had on me, he'd want to eat out every day of the week. Jonathan hadn't seen it in me. It turns me on when a man takes me to dinner. Just the idea of it makes me hot inside. I'm so busy cooking, I rarely eat out. I love it when *he* picks the restaurant and dresses for the occasion, and when he orders for me. After what I've told him I want, of course, and I can just sit there, little ol' demure me and feel smug and taken care of. I usually look down and smile. Sometimes I have to close my eyes and have a private moment over it. I love it when he leaves a good tip. There's something so powerful in the gesture.

I had nearly exhausted my short list of hopefuls from Great Expectations when Simon and I talked on the phone. I took the call at my office. I didn't really want to bring anyone home so soon, so to speak.

"Lip Service."

"Hello, is Gwen there?"

I like the voice, whoever he is.

"This is Gwen."

"This is Simon. The lovely women at Great Expectations just gave me permission to call you and make our first contact."

"Oh. Hello." I'd only told them he could yesterday. He's on it. Does that mean attentive all-round? I stand suddenly and reach all the way to my office door with the phone cord following. I close it gently. No need for one-sided eavesdropping from my kitchen staff.

"Hiiii," he says, dragging it out like pulled molasses.

"Hi," I say. Mine is dreamier. I know what he looks like. He's the closest thing I'd ever seen to a Greek God. With short curly dark hair close-cropped to his scalp and olive-colored skin, he would look amazing in a tuxedo.

"So what brand of Lip Service are you in the business of providing?"

Ooh, good question for me of all people. Cunning too. "I cater to the needs of my clients."

"Ooh, elusive, yet direct. Is that something you might do over lunch or dinner?"

"Yes. It is."

I wonder if he's trying to psyche me out.

"I think we should have dinner then. Soon. Are you free tonight?"

*Ooh. Yes, please!*

By the time our conversation is over, I know he's smart, hard-working, expressive—which I am looking forward to—and successful. He's a senior executive at Bloen & Blotnik, an advertising company I'd catered for once. If memory served me, I'd done a power lunch for them there. With lots of protein on their plates. Where was he then, I wondered. He undoubtedly wore a suit to work. Bloen & Blotnik did not believe in dress-down days in the workplace. I thought he'd look good in a suit, maybe even out of it. I am intrigued. He even makes me laugh. And I'm not laughing at him. I'm laughing with him.

I open my office door to see Georgina waiting there, ears peeled.

"Keep your legs together and *don't* take your skirt *off*," she says to me.

The nerve.

*!!***!!***!!*

I WRAP things up at work early so I can take my time bathing and dressing. I clip my toenails, file my fingernails down to nothing, cream my cuticles. Peppermint lotion lands on my feet, a fragrant after-bath splashes my legs. Perfumed lotion around my midriff and up and down my arms—a double dose on my elbows. Nothing on my neck. In the event a kiss falls there, I want him to taste nothing but clean fresh flesh. Perfume around my hairline, behind my ears and knees. I put a ring on and a bracelet.

I search through my closet, one garment at a time, for the right dress to set an impression. Something elegant, yet daring.

Something with the sleek, yet full-bodied feminine approach I am hoping for. Something, something, something. Aha! I find all that and *more* in my off-the-shoulder, full-length Adrienne Vittadini dress with a flared bottom that swooshes around my ankles as I turn corners, then circles in it, practicing. My insides stir with the idea that someone might like the way I look in it. I feel good in it. The icing on the cake is the Evan Picone shoes on my manicured feet.

Simon takes me to Ivy at the Shore in Santa Monica. He surrenders the car to the valet guy—part of the excitement for me. His hand touches my back before I sit down and I am wet with anticipation before the menus are thrust into our hands.

Simon orders the fillet mignon. I want to taste it from his mouth, but we hardly know each other. That would be inappropriate, I chide myself in the privacy of my own head. But I don't complain when he pushes the fork to my face and offers a piece to me.

I can hardly refuse. I snatch that meat quicker than he expects but he is openly amused.

He is thoughtful with his food. He takes his time with it and eats at his own pace. He doesn't mix the mashed potatoes with the creamed corn he has on the side. He lets every flavor mingle only with his taste buds. I sit, captivated by his approach, forgetting that I'd been eating at all.

Before I know it, the waiter drops off our check. He reaches for it without hesitation, takes a quick look at it, digs into his pockets (I'd have done that for him), and pulls out a wad of cash. Thumbs through it, pulls some bills, throws them on the table, and says, "I'd like to take you to the beach now."

Ooh, such command.

"Okay." I am practically speechless.

I have him on his knees before the night is over.

Simon says, "Let me kiss you."

Ha! I let him kiss me when we're at the beach. He asks so politely. He looks so cute sitting there on his mini lawn chair, fumbling with the champagne bottle he produced from the mini ice chest, his chiseled profile turned toward me. I watch him—stunned that he'd thought so far ahead. I avoided answering him at first. I didn't know if I wanted to go there. I remember I'm trying to turn over a new leaf here. No jumping in too fast and finding myself naked and in the arms of a stranger so soon I tell myself. No more of the shut-up and kiss me approach. Well at least *he'd* kissed *me.* I find him irresistible. I cannot refuse him.

He kisses me again. This time I kiss back. I taste his champagne mouth, a virtual toast to the tongue.

"Oh, you're my kind of girl," he says.

"What kind is that?" I ask.

"Sumptuous. Delicious." He squeezes his hands over mine and lingers there. "I had a great time," he says as he drops me off at my house with one last kiss to send me on my way.

I knew I would have to have him.

By the time I go to bed—alone—my thoughts are swimming with Simon. No wonder. My tongue had been swimming all night. We may as well have still been at the beach.

I toss and turn for hours, images of my hopeful future tossing along with me. I am a fiery hellcat. Simon is on top of me whispering in my ear—tell me, tell me what you want, goddess of love. *Take me,* I say. *I want to take you now*, he says. *Take me anywhere, take me nowhere, just take me*, I say. The sheets are perfumed, and we wrap ourselves in the intoxicating scent as it mixes with our salty-sweet flesh.

He keeps his mouth to my ear telling me how much he wants me and what he wants to do to me. *You're so sumptuous*, he says.

I moan and turn to bite his ear as I come and come, my toes curling and breasts rising to press into him. What a wet, wet dream.

*!!***!!***!!*

SIMON CALLS the next morning, confident he'll get another date.

"Hello, Gwen," he practically whispers, "that was lip-smacking service last night. I went home happily hungry for more."

I am desperately trying to take it slow. Fat chance that's going to happen, but I am trying to, at least.

"I'm having a dinner party on Wednesday night if you'd like to come." I haven't planned anything at all, but I have good reason to now. Better to be in a crowd with Simon than alone. Strength in numbers, and all that.

"Will it be just the two of us?"

"Us and a few others sprinkled in for interest."

I hang up with him and start dialing.

My dinner parties are events extraordinaire. Something my friends clear their schedules for. Fine china, cloth napkins, centerpieces to set the mood. I rarely cook anything off my already established menu for friends. Way too easy. Instead I risk their opinion of me and plan to try something I've never done before. This time a new menu I pulled from the dog-eared cookbooks still lying by my bed. Better to try a new menu on my guests than my discerning clientele.

I am tempted to invite just my new would-be boyfriends to this dinner party, enjoying the fantasy of what that might be like. In my vision they all look confused. I am not feeling all that nervy, thinking I better do the boy-girl-boy-girl thing. My reasons are two-fold. It would be good if one or two of my friends could meet my prospective specimen of a man and give me their opinion of him—and no doubt, I need a chaperone. It is clear to me I would need one or I'd unequivocally end up in bed with him way too soon.

I am bound to overlook negative character traits in favor of extreme physical beauty. So I enlist the help of my dear friend Genevieve. I met her at an Indian cooking class a few years back. She has a taste for the exotic, although she was born in France, and she has a good palette when it comes to testing new recipes. I love to share them with her.

"Come early. Keep me company as they start to show up." There's a good possibility I'll grab one of the boys and undress him if she isn't there in time to stop me. I do not want to be held responsible for my actions no matter how responsible I am or how hard I try.

Genevieve is single and always on the prowl, although she'll never admit it. She likes to think she goes out because there's something to do. Really she goes out because there's someone to find. She is highly motivated in getting first pick at my dating left-overs and getting as much bang out of my buck as she can muster. She's got beauty going for her, a deep strawberry blonde bob with bangs that always hangs perfectly. A cute little waist and a happy disposition make her really appealing on the surface.

Georgina wants to see the results of my homework assignment, so I let her come too.

"I promise not to leave until all the boys have gone home," Georgina says decisively. "Philip is hoping to catch the Lakers game at El Cholo with the rest of the guys anyway."

A halibut dish I'd never tried and a summer terrine I was boldly attempting without all the called-for ingredients are my main course. I am so not pressured by substituting broccoli for the recommended cauliflower. I wouldn't be letting Georgina know, though, or she'd take on the worry for me and make me nervous through osmosis. She'd check the oven continuously and wouldn't be focused on helping me choose the right guy.

It's a soothing endeavor to be in my own kitchen at home—a scaled-down version of my professional environment complete with silver tables, countertops, and a six-burner Wolf gas stove I may never part with. The parmesan and nut-encrusted halibut is seared by the time the girls arrive. Popping it in the oven ten minutes before I want to serve is all I have to do.

Genevieve is the first to arrive, not so much because I had asked her to come early, but because she likes to watch me in action and hopes to demystify my expertise. She keeps her eyes and ears on me without the distraction of my other guests. It's not unlike her to unwrap my folded napkins slowly and try to refold them the way I had to test her own ability. She does all of this casually, thinking I don't notice.

"So, who's coming?" she asks, already smoothing out her vest, and straightening the white blouse peeking from under it, brushing it smooth against her pencil skirt.

"Jonathan the salesman, Dan the sailorman, and Simon the man oh man."

"So, Simon's the one you like?"

"They're all perfectly likable, Genevieve. You'll see."

I grab a napkin and show her how to do the napkin fanning and still make it stand up on the plate. She gets it her first try. She's empowered.

Georgina arrives shortly after and before any of the men did.

"Now how did you do that?" Genevieve asks of the terrine. "I wish you'd teach me how to make it." She is awed by my menu as always.

"Oh, anyone can do it."

Jonathan and Dan arrive next. It is seeing Simon that makes me flustered. I kept thinking about the way he tipped the waiter the other night.

Dan kisses me hello and shakes hands with Genevieve, and Georgina, who were already at the door. They line up like knowing mothers smiling politely, but shrewdly aware of what a man could do to hurt their little darling. Jonathan looks confused. I don't know any of these guys enough to warrant them getting possessive with me.

I'd instructed the girls not to waste time on questions about how we'd all met. I don't want the boys to know about the connection of Great Expectations. Dan's wearing jeans and a thick belt with a nautical buckle. Genevieve is captivated by his stormy weather on the sea stories. Before I serve dessert, Dan suggests Genevieve sail with him sometime soon. She knows I hear him ask and gives me a quick look asking for my permission. Why would I stop her? I know if I were really looking for a marriage, I'd choose someone with similar lifestyle choices, so we'd have more to work with.

Jonathan and Simon are instant friends. Jonathan's sales expertise and Simon's ability to sell concepts through advertising are a good mix. They both like playing racquetball.

They both dress up for work. They talk about everything under the sun including how delicious dinner is. While Simon isn't overly demonstrative, there are looks in my direction often. He is talking with the others, but highly aware of my presence.

The terrine is passed from person to person, as is the halibut.

Once Georgina gets her food in front of her, her own agenda kicks in. She starts asking pointed questions of them all, trying to garner an opinion before the night is over.

"So, Jonathan, what are your plans for the immediate future?"

"Well, we're looking to increase our sales 30 percent this year at which time I'll be taking an extra week's vacation and coming back refreshed to kick our sales team all the way to the top. I plan on being with the company for the long haul. I like the stability. They treat me right."

"And Simon, what about you?"

I don't hear his answer. I'm busy in the kitchen with coffee and tea.

Dan suggests he walk Genevieve to her car as things are wrapping up. Jonathan and Simon leave shortly after. Georgina stays long enough to help put plates into the dishwasher.

Simon comes back to my house shortly after Georgina leaves. His knock is deliberate. I can imagine him in a meeting he's leading. He would be direct. To the point. He would get things done. The knock says it's him. I open the door, stand in the doorway so he can't rush in so soon. I need to consider this. The girls are gone and if I know them, their calls are coming in shortly. We have to go over the entire evening. I expect them to be objective and then predictive.

"I want to thank you for inviting me for dinner."

"Oh, good, then you liked it."

"Loved it."

I hadn't let go of the doorknob yet. He is stepping closer nonetheless.

"Can I help clean up? I'm sure there's something I can do."

*Yeah. Lick the crumbs off my face.*

"Help you wash the dishes or wrap leftovers or something." He moves closer to me with his mouth close to my ear. "Maybe then you'd tell me the secret of your terrine. All those layers stacked up on top of each other like that, mixing their flavors and yet keeping their distance—and so colorful. It was light and yet full-bodied." He is playful now.

The phone rings. Who knows who? Who cares why? I'm not going to reach for it.

"How'd you like the halibut?" I am opening the door now—an involuntary action similar to breathing. He can pass now and be in here with me. "Did you find it moist enough?"

"Well, you can't just say it was light, or just moist, or just perfect. You'd have to say perfectly moist and light. In fact, forget wrapping the leftovers. Let's have seconds instead. I like cold seconds, no need to warm mine again."

He is in the kitchen now, searching, rifling through the cupboards for plates and clean forks. Putting a plate together for me. I butter his bread for him.

"Such good nibbles," he says before he leans over to try my neck. His lips are there now, commanding. I close my eyes. Then I feel the cold terrine against my lips. My mouth opens. He keeps his fingers in my mouth while I lick my way around the taste of terrine-flavored fingers. I sleep with him. Maybe a little too soon. Probably too soon. I'm kicking myself now, but not really. It takes two to tango, and we dance all night. The future is unclear and I am not a virgin. We spend the entire next day together. We go for a lazy midmorning brunch and then go right back to bed, exploring the outer reaches of each other until dawn. So hard to pull apart and resume our separate lives.

I feel his energy in my body all day long like squiggly spaghetti. *What if?* What if I ruined it already by letting him have access to my treasure chest? *What if?* What if he loves me so much, he asks me to marry him? *What if?* What if I love him enough to say yes? Is that a fate worse than death? I am serious when I ask myself this question. Death is a transition. Most would agree there is life after death. But marriage is permanent. Even an impermanent marriage leaves permanent scars.

Georgina isn't any help with this. I'd been trying to reach her all morning. Sure, she was anxious to get the ball rolling for me, but now that I was in the thick of it, I couldn't find her. I need her advice and I need to know if she needs me to pick anything up before I drive to the kitchen.

My doubts escalate. What if this plays itself out for five, six months, or two or three years of my adult life and nothing comes of it? I'm aging in dog years here. Living in the moment, letting life stretch before me is fine if my next birthday made me twenty-three but I'll be nearly forty in not so many years. Life's moments have long become life's memories and my clock is ticking.

I run to the farmers market for the fresh fruit I use in the tarts, the only missing ingredient for Shelly's bridal shower menu and grab myself a bouquet of flowers in a get-well soon, well-meaning way. Like I fell sick or something. I dropped the fruit off but find the kitchen empty. Then I go home alone to my empty house, full of the evidence of our time together.

Before I even turn a light on, I lift my phone receiver to check for messages. Zero. Zip. Nothing. Ugh. I have no appetite although I open the refrigerator door to see if anything feels right. I have no desire to make anything. I've made a mess of my life already. I just know it.

The next day Georgina and I are packing the tarts in bakery boxes and loading them into the Lip-Mobile and trying to catch up at the same time. She's not impressed when she hears my Simon says diatribe. She's busting my chops about it willingly. "Well, you're the tart with heart, aren't you? That was sneaky of him to come back," she says. I hear her huffing. Not supportive of it whatsoever. I know she's getting back at me for my remark about her maybe never marriage to Philip. She's already been living with him for a year and wedding plans are not forthcoming. It's a touchy subject. I gingerly place the delicate phyllo nests in the safest place and let it go.

Shelly's mother excels at her job and delivers her surprised daughter to Allison's just after the buffet is ready. When Shelly, the bride-to-be, sees us at the front door, she says, "Oh, you're in on this too, are you?" She gives me a quick kiss on the cheek, as if we're friends. I really want to do her wedding.

I doubt that Shelly Van Buren had given it up too soon. Maybe she didn't even like sex and that was why she was engaged. Her soon-to-be husband, Adam, probably respected the heck out of her. She was neat. A tidy little package herself, I thought, as I watched her with her presents. Her clothes had fine lines. I envied Shelly her happiness, seeing her friends and family around her in a show of support. I wanted it too. All the smiles and laughs and warm embraces. I wouldn't mind the new Cuisinart either. Her ring catches light from the living room window and looks like the call from a lighthouse. Yes, I see it. I am cast away at sea and need her light to guide me in.

She'll probably make a great wife, although I'm worrying whether he'll be getting enough. I want to be a wife to someone. "I'm a wife. I'm a wife," I try that out loud in the privacy of the kitchen to see how it sounds and how it feels to me. Georgina hears me but I am unashamed and press on. I want to be the wife of a husband. My husband. I have a husband. "Oh, husband! Oh, husband! It is your loving wife!" I want to help take care of someone too. I do want to cook great dinners and clean up after him. I do. I can't help it. Holiday dinners. Everything.

I am determined to keep in touch with both these women. They inspire me, give me hope, and with any luck, will pay me large amounts of money to cater for them. I'm getting to know them well enough to know what they like. Even why they like it.

I catch Shelly alone at the buffet table. She's not reaching for anything to eat. She's just standing there looking at everything.

She looks a little lost and I want to hug her. When she notices me, she says, "Well, you've been baking your heart out. Look at all those hearts. They're everywhere."

"I want to help you," I say.

"Oh," she says skeptically.

"I want to teach you some dishes. Some basics of cooking that will be a good foundation for your life with Adam."

"Oh!" she says, less skeptically now.

"We don't even have to tell Adam. Why don't we schedule something? I'll come to you."

"Maybe I should come to you," she says, conspiratorially. "I wouldn't want Adam to know I'm so inept."

"Oh, he's not going to know a thing."

*!!***!!***!!*

I ASK Georgina, "Is it okay to call him? I mean can I call Simon and ask him what he ate for breakfast this morning? I just want a few words of connection."

She advises, "Do not pursue him. It is poor dating etiquette. Let the man have time to miss you and seek you out. You're so impatient. Why are you in such a rush anyway? If you think happily ever after is possible with this man, then prolong the inevitable. The beginning of a relationship is delicate and magical. Let it grow slowly. If I were a botanist, I'd tell you not to overwater your plant or expose it to too much sun. You'll kill it. Don't be so obsessively needy."

"I'll have to tie my hands together to keep myself from calling Simon and asking him why he hasn't called me."

"The problem with women is that we experience time differently than men. Our calendars move much faster. A day for a man is like a month for a woman. Agonizing. It's more painful to be in love than not. It's much better to let him set his trap. Men need mating to be a primordial game—the hunt, the challenge, and all that. It took me years to get that. Don't waste your time. You can't try that hard. If he's not calling you, and isn't in hot pursuit of you, you're not calling him."

"It's just so difficult to be passive."

"What's it been? Twelve hours?"

"It's been forever. I wish I hadn't slept with him so soon."

I hit the binders at Great Expectations again. I convince myself that if I date other men, I keep myself from getting in over my head with Simon.

Simon says, "Call me back." Finally! I play his message over and over. "Call me back. I want to take you to dinner Friday night." I waited until the end of the day to call him back. I'm practically dying.

He takes me out for dinner, his tie loosens over cappuccino, then he suggests he take me home to my bedroom. Hook, line, and sinker. Who says no to this. The word does not exist in my vocabulary. I am so already there. Cannot wait to bed him again.

*!!***!!***!!*

I LIKE watching him. The way his pants fall against his legs. The way he opens the trunk to his car. The way his wet hair is flattened against his head after a shower. I like him so much I underline the days that I see him on my wall calendar. Simon. Every moment is so special I want to keep track of it all.

I love our walks on the beach. I feel like a woman when I am with him. He's so much a man and complements me so well. His energy seeps into me. I wear my long skirts and heeled shoes and laugh a lighter laugh when I am with him. I feel like a monogamous Aphrodite. I am impassioned and emblazoned with lust and eroticism.

Simon says, "I want to see you play with yourself." We're in bed again. It's funny how men want you to play with yourself so they can watch, like it brings them such pleasure to do so. My thoughts on the subject are this. I've been playing with myself for more than two years already. I finally manage to get a man in my bed so the last thing I want to do is play touchy-feely with myself. Believe me. I explain this to Simon but not in so many words. I suggest we let it be something for him to look forward to another time.

He answers, "Well, I guess I'll have to play with you."

"Please do."

I feel taken care of. He is thinking of ways he can bring me happiness. I am thinking of ways I can receive him graciously. I like to let him take the lead. It makes me feel like more of a woman. I have painted my toenails red because of him and have contemplated wearing more makeup. We are bonding and getting closer by the day.

*!!***!!***!!*

I LET Shelly come to my kitchen for her cooking lessons. She looks small and out of place here. "Let's start with this steak recipe. Men get such hard-ons for big slabs of meat. This is really easy to prepare. Just measure equal parts of soy sauce and honey, mix it together and use it as a marinade. Salt and pepper the steaks lightly, pour the marinade over, and let them baste for a while—overnight is great. You sear them and then bake them off—but don't overbake them. Not everyone likes tough beef."

"Try to make it sound easy, Gwen."

"It is easy. All you need are a few signature dishes—with a few simple variations here and there and you'll give him the impression you have an endless repertoire. Believe me, when he tries this meat, he'll want it all the time—he'll be singing your praises for years to come."

# Chapter Five

## Holten Sails Company Picnic

Menu for 200
Southwestern Barbecue Ribs
Meaty Meat Burgers with Cucumber Relish
Blue Cheese Turkey Burgers with Red Pepper Salsa
Kasha Veggie Burgers, Chili Dogs
Corn on the Cob, Creamy Potato Salad
Spicy Slaw
Cake & Ice Cream

The path is narrowing. Any chance I have at keeping myself open to other relationships is instantly thwarted when Jonathan calls to cancel our preplanned and confirmed Saturday night date. The universe seems to be working with me on this one. Maybe I have a good chance at monogamy after all. He calls to say he locked his keys in his bedroom and he won't be able to leave until someone comes with another key. Every sense I have tells me he is lying and what a lame excuse to get out of a date.

"You're welcome to come down here," he says into the phone.

"What, and crawl through your window?"

"Well, another time then if you want."

I remind myself that one of the reasons I blew him off last weekend, aside from it interfering with my date with Simon, was because he wanted me to go down to Hermosa Beach and meet him there. I just don't travel on the first few dates. That's way too available on my part and a sign of laziness on the man's part.

Georgina agrees. We prefer to have the man come and get me. "Who's pursuing whom here?" she says repeatedly.

So maybe the universe is clearing my path. Obliterating any chance of sabotaging the goodness I have called into my life. Let's remember the dating crisis I had during my first week of responses and the power-dating overwhelm I experienced. I am nervous, however, about narrowing my focus on only one man.

I am also nervous about the Holten Sails event too. The location for their upcoming picnic is not secured. The great debate over whether to choose Will Rogers State Park or Franklin Canyon Park has been going on for weeks already, the clients fighting their own internal battles while I wait it out on the sidelines, poised for action. While Will Rogers offers a view of the Pacific Ocean and appeals to the senior members of the Holten Sails board, the younger, more progressive members want it at Franklin Canyon Park. They want to hoist a few sailboats right into the tiny lake there and serve drinks from the decks, toasting their greatest year yet.

No one explains how the guests are to get from boat to boat. No one has decided whether they are toasting their toasts with real glassware or plastic throw-away cups. The event is less than a week away. I try not to let their indecision stop me from ordering what I need from my vendors and start my prep list. At least they approve of my menu.

This was too big a job for Georgina and me to be cleaning up after ourselves so I arrange for Carlos to come and wash dishes. I hadn't used him in a while, and he needed the work. I might have used him sooner but he becomes territorial in my kitchen. Forget about trying to wash my own knife with Carlos around. I'm guilty if I even think of going near his domain.

He says to me from the get-go, feeling he must remind me in case I've forgotten, "I am the dishwasher. You are the chef. I take care of what's in the sink, you take care of what's on the stove."

Dishwashers, I have learned in not so easy ways, are a temperamental lot. The first to not stand the heat in the kitchen. They demand pay raises more frequently and resent having to do anything with food before it's been eaten. He is already put off by the roasted red peppers cooling in the sink, their black skins making a mess of it already. "Sorry, Carlos, sometimes I forget it's my kitchen."

I'm dicing the potatoes I'm going to need for my potato salad while lost in the love song that's playing in my head. Simon. Simon. Simon. Maybe I'll marry Simon. I make three lengthwise cuts along the russet potato and then dice, dice, dice. I look down and see that part of my thumbnail is missing. I look at the pile of potatoes set aside in their water bath and know it'll be too hard to find. I search for it anyway feeling compelled to at least try. I drain the potatoes through the colander and refill the rinse water. Nothing. I give up my search, cynically amused that they're getting more than they paid for if the nail didn't wash away. Maybe I'll find it once the potatoes have been boiled.

It is hot in the kitchen. Even with the fans blowing and the back-gated door open for added circulation, I am hot enough to be happy I'd worn a short cotton dress. I soak a bandana in ice water, then wrap it around my head. A big pot of my chili is simmering on the stove. It has been there for hours already. I try it and decide it's perfect. I turn the burner off to let it cool, not that it helps any of us cool off.

The pressure mounts as the day progresses. Carlos whistles while he works. I ask him repeatedly to stop but he has no idea he is whistling at all and answers indignantly each time, "I am not whistling." He is grating on my nerves. We're having a tug of war with the radio station too. Every time I leave the kitchen and enter my office, I hear the static between stations as he turns the button from 93.1 to his preferred Spanish radio station. And back to whistling he goes.

Georgina keeps quiet. I see she doesn't want to pick sides. Pissing Carlos off by taking my side may push him out the door before the dishes are done, and she has tired of doing dishes. I debate on turning Emeril Live on louder than Emeril himself and tuning

Carlos out altogether. *Bam!* Take that. I close the door between the kitchen and my office instead, take a few deep breaths, and dial my client. Still no word about the location, and from what I can tell, no concern on their part whatsoever about where in this city I'd be feeding them. Maybe they know about the food gods and know we would materialize the event as quickly as the fifth day of creation.

"So, what if the rental company doesn't know where they'll be taking the two four-foot barbecues, or the thirty-six-inch diameter round tables, or the blue and white tablecloths to go on them, or the padded chairs people should be sitting on." I mumble this under my breath like I am eating the distaste of it all and want to spit it out.

There is no one to take it out on, so I ask Carlos to mop the floor spotless when he finishes with the dishes. I call my request from the door of my office. While Spanish is his mother tongue, he does understand any statement that incorporates words relating to clean, to wash, to mop, to shine. If I asked him to make the concrete shine like a newborn baby's bum, he'd have the mop and pail out before I completed my sentence. I guess if he wanted to whistle his way across the floor I'd have to concede. Georgina came to let me know they were wrapping up for the day.

"Do you want me to put the chili away?" she asks. "It's cool enough."

"No, I'm coming. I'll do it."

I open the door of the refrigerator and clear a space for it on a shelf. I pick the pot up off the burner and turn with it, heading for the fridge. The open door swings shut just as I am reaching for the shelf and I knock my elbow enough to set myself off balance. I lose hold of the right handle and down the pot goes, the contents spilling onto the floor Carlos just made pristine.

Without a word, Georgina and I are both squatting to salvage all that's possible to by spooning it back into the pot with cupped hands—not all of it. Just the top layer. If we act quickly it would be like it never happened. If Carlos hadn't just mopped the floor,

I'd be making a whole new pot. I'm ready to close the door on this day by the time it ends.

The next day doesn't get much easier. The location still eludes me. Carlos continues to whistle. I ask him to stop. He approaches me later, invading my physical space. He comes up so close, I have to back up just to keep some distance. He looks at me for a moment, and asks, "If I can't whistle, then why are you humming?"

"I'm not humming."

"You're humming."

"I am?" He's right. I *am* humming. He caught me. "Okay, so whistle Dixie for all I care." I hide in my office for the rest of the morning, safe from Carlos.

There are staff to rally together for this barbecue so I get on the phone to book the assortment of culinary wannabes and out-of-work actors I keep in touch with so staffing parties is easier. I have to call them all back once the location is determined.

By the time I am ready to get my hands dirty with rib prep and burger making the day is nearly over. Carlos does an excellent job cleaning out the refrigerator and erasing any tell-tale signs of my chili accident the previous day. He eyes the chili pot on the shelf, "Do you want me to throw this away?"

"No. Leave it where it is," I reply, not bothered by what he may think of me if I go ahead and serve it. "You're good to go, Carlos. I'll see you tomorrow."

Georgina makes good progress with the potato salad and spicy slaw. She even manages to find my missing thumbnail piece, spotting it easily. I'd warned her to keep an eye out for it. Big sigh of relief.

I want the soothing task of shucking the corn, but she is well underway with the dozens of ears, their husks and silk piled high in the garbage pail beside her. She cleans herself up when she is through and is off.

Simon comes to my kitchen on his way home from work. He catches me mixing blue cheese into the ground turkey with my hands when he arrives. I have my plastic gloves on. He stands in the doorway and watches.

"Is that a secret recipe you're working on?" he asks, his hand casually resting against the doorframe like he wouldn't think of coming near me like that, but taunting me with the threat of it.

"Yeah, it's a secret, all right. As secret as my chili recipe. You best keep your distance," I say mockingly. He knows me well enough already to keep a safe distance while I was working in the kitchen.

"I want you," he says as he walks around my island, overstepping my boundaries. He stands behind me, rubbing up against my back.

"I had a really hard day," he says, pushing his hard-on into me. "It was hard thinking about you all day."

"Oh, yeah?" I keep working the ground turkey, my insides turning moist.

He reaches across me for a squeeze of the blue cheese and pops it in his mouth. He reaches across for another one, resting it against my lips. I look at him before I open my mouth and let him push it inside.

I feel the cotton of my dress stretching and lifting from behind and then feel his hand suddenly between my legs. The ties of my apron loosen and his teeth are on the back of my neck. He finishes his bite with a smack of his lips and then comes back for more. The turkey and blue cheese mix just fine.

"I'm not usually into raw meat, but you sure have me tempted," he says, his breath in my ear.

The call from Mr. Holten himself comes as we are coming. I hear his voice on the recorder in my office saying they'd decided after great debate—no kidding—on Franklin Canyon Park and to please confirm the venue is still available.

*Oh, yes, oh, yes, oh.*

*!!***!!***!!*

I TALK the Holten board members out of toasting from the sailboats. There just isn't enough time to build a plank from the shore of the lake to the boat, or hire extra staff to row rubber dinghies full of people just to toast in celebration. Not to mention the extra liability required for such a maneuver. I convince them the president is better off doing his speech from the bow of the sailboat while staff members gather on the shore with glasses raised. All food is being served onshore.

The day of the event, I set up a makeshift kitchen right there in the park complete with portable refrigeration, propane stoves, warming ovens, and lots and lots of tabletop surrounded by a tent with walls so we'd have our privacy. I have the girls prepping the salads there while the guys come in and out for instructions on how to move the food around and which tables to display on. There are two guys on each barbecue and a floating man with a spatula.

"What are you doing with that spatula?" one of the girls asks him.

"Flippin' the flippin' burgers," he says.

Georgina directs the crowd to the various stations. "Barbecue straight ahead, salad and fixins to your right, dessert behind you."

"Have you got all the fixins for the burgers?" I hear someone ask as I am floating between stations, and then Georgina's voice again, "Barbecue straight ahead, salad and fixins to your right, dessert behind you."

Georgina takes a break once all the guests have been through the line at least once and eats a hot dog under the tent.

"Oh, that looks good," Michele, one of my waitstaff, says. "I've been thinking about a chili dog all day."

"Take a pass on the chili," she suggests to Michele without explanation.

I watch an obese woman and her chunky daughter eyeing the lineup for the cake. Their hands fidget with plates already smeared with icing from their first helping.

"Fat people scare me. They'll just eat and eat and eat. They're always the ones going for the ice cream and cake."

No doubt the cake's good. There are more than a dozen people within easy reach of me that are doing their best to stay away from it. I can tell by the looks on their faces. I can read that look of itchy discomfort they transmit while exercising their self-control. Some are buckling under the pressure. It's a picnic after all.

"Ok. Let them eat cake," I say aloud.

The event was a huge success. Mr. Holten himself thanks me while he eats his second turkey-blue burger. Mustard falls to his plate. He wipes his mouth quickly, efficiently. No wonder his company enjoys so much success. He has great command over everything.

"Let's do this again next year, Ms. Devine. Everything was divine!" With that he winks at me.

Around the time the barbecue is cooling off, he gives me a huge kiss on the cheek, smiling, and a quick pinch on my rear. He takes another bite of his burger, while sun bounces off his face. "Yes, we'll definitely do this again."

# Chapter Six

## Wynn Zimmerman Cocktail Party

Tray-passed Hors d'Oeuvres Menu for 100
Shrimp Cocktail Shots
Mini Kebabs with Pearl Onion and Mixed Olives
Mini Chicken Salad Bread Boxes
Crème Fraiche & Caviar Filled Potato Shells

Simon and I continue to see each other. At every angle. Georgina is charting our progress and checking things off our prep list too—all while roasting peppers on the range and chopping vegetables for salad. Our to-do list is getting done but it is so hot in the kitchen, all the little fans in the corners are going.

"And the sex? How is it?" she asks.

"Fantasy sex."

"So, it's good?"

"Who fantasizes about bad sex? Of course, it's good."

"So, you've got a boy toy."

"More like a boy with toys."

"Buy all the toys and accoutrements you want now and have lots of fun doing it. Have him take you to Frederick's and he can watch you try everything on."

"It's become one of our favorite outings. If we aren't in the mood to drive the distance to Hollywood, we settle on short trips to Victoria's Secret on the West Side."

"That's nice, but I wouldn't narrow my options with Simon so soon, if I were you."

"I shouldn't put all my eggs in one basket? Is that what you're saying?"

"In case he's the type to never give up his toys and get beyond the play stage. I think you should keep looking."

I haven't promised anything to Simon and he certainly hasn't professed his undying love for me. The last time he spewed himself into me he said, "Oh! So good, so good, so good. Oh!" before collapsing against me, spent. So I decide Georgina is right.

*!!***!!***!!*

STILL TECHNICALLY a free agent, I find myself back in the selection chamber. I decide to flip through the R binder because R is for Robert. I'd already said yes to his request for a night out, and I want to refresh my memory by rereading his profile. I take one look at his picture and decide R is for ravishing Mr. Right. I remember he is the scientist. A tall, dark, and handsome man through anyone's eyes. I read on. He likes browsing in bookstores, movies on rainy days, and eating anything that's good. He has a master's in atmospheric science. *Hey, baby, check out my atmosphere*, I say to myself while reading his profile in the selection chamber. Oh, I notice, he finds humor in everyday life. *How funny, so do I.* He is looking for *an electrochemically compatible woman to create a nest of love,* to quote him exactly. He's an acceptable specimen of a date as far as I can see.

*!!***!!***!!*

WYNN ZIMMERMAN Advertising calls me every year for their annual cocktail party, and this year is no different, I learn, when I'm back in my office. Georgina is the bearer of good news.

"I talked to Wynn Zimmerman himself," she says excitedly. "He wants to hear from you pronto. He's landed some really big clients this year, so he wants their party to be bigger and better than last year. He used the 'c' word."

"Caviar?" I ask.

"That 'c' exactly."

This makes me nervous. Not the fact that I'd be doing a party for a public relations firm—the fact that I'd have to be in a room full of PR men, publicly relating to them. I had a tête-à-tête with one of them, Steve, last year, and he still works there. I had crossed into dangerous territory with him then, but there is no saying no to Wynn Zimmerman. There is no saying no to Steve either, probably.

*!!***!!***!!*

ROBERT SEEMS like a perfect gentleman and since he lives close enough to me and he's not driving out of his way, I concede to let him pick me up at my place. Although that could be a tricky maneuver when returning after our date, I feel I can trust myself. I feel this false sense of security when I am in my house alone. I am so sure, so confident, even as I open the door when he rings my bell. Then I see him. In the flesh. He is real, carrying enough body around to tempt all my senses. My body involuntarily pushes itself toward him and I trip, my foot awkwardly meeting the threshold of my front door. He catches me before I fall. His curly black hair contrasts with the salt and pepper stubble on his cheeks.

"That was close," he says, so capable of catching me.

"Wasn't it though?" I agree, softly.

We drive across town with the top down and a warm current of air hits us as we slice through it. In my head, I am a virtual tour of questions. *What am I doing? Who is this man? How does he fit in? What? Why? How? When?* And on and on and on. At some point I decide he's perfect for me.

He's talkative, too, but I haven't heard a thing. I'm just smiling, stupidly.

Later, at the end of the night, we drive back along the empty streets with the top up. The glistening streetlamps give the scene a surreal air. R is for restraint and trying really hard not to ravish Mr. Right rapidly. I want to make love to him.

Any quasi-loyalty to Simon born out of our short time together is waning. Now if Simon *had* professed his undying love, Georgina needn't have talked me into this date. At least that's what I tell myself.

My skin is alive. I am bubbling up from the inside and want to spill over into the night. My nagging loyalty, not surprisingly to Simon but to myself, prevents me from doing anything other than hugging Robert in my driveway. It is the longest hug I've ever hugged. *Maybe he's debating whether to make a move. Maybe he's waiting for me to do something.* In the past I'd have hurried things along. *I* forgo the idea of jumping *him*, a thought that shocks even me.

If something is going to happen, he'll have to reach out and grab more than just my shoulders. It's his move to make, and he'll be the one to blame for making it. He doesn't make a move though. Not feeling frisky? No initiative? No doubt my succumbing to him leads to coming with him. In a split second.

Instead he says, "What a nice hug," and holds me tighter. "I'd like to see you again."

"I'd like that."

"I'll call you soon." He retreats, his graceful gait and sweet smile holding me there at the door. I go inside, but not before I watch his every move down my street.

*!!***!!***!!*

HOPEFULLY THIS isn't a bad omen or anything, but I don't have enough staff to work the Wynn Zimmerman cocktail party. Some of the girls I planned to use in the scullery station canceled, two of my best waitstaff had unwittingly double-booked themselves, and none of my easy reach support staff were anywhere to be found. And because I sold Wynn on letting us do a big-budget theme party, Georgina is way deep in decorating and setting the scene.

"Just when we're stretching into décor packages with props. Not a good omen. We need to get Chef Mate on this," she says.

"I'll call. You pray."

"It's pretty last minute."

"I'm going to start taking it personally if anyone else cancels."

Carlos hears us griping when he comes in from the parking lot. He's been cleaning and reorganizing the Lip-Mobile to allow room for food and props. "I have cousins. They can help."

"Yeah?'

I give him a chair nearest the phone so his fingers can do the walking. One of his cousins answers right away. We go from English to Spanish and back again giving job descriptions and other pertinent details, and two of his cousins are immediately on board before any sweat breaks my brow. Relief. He translates directions to them over the phone.

"Two down. Two to go." In a few minutes we'd be in our eleventh hour.

"Chef Mate is going to come through for us," Georgina determines.

The food prep for the Wynn Zimmerman party is easy enough. Tray-passed hors d'oeuvres, best prepared ahead of time, are assembled and placed on platters on-site. Georgina and I pack everything up and are ready to make our way through traffic to their offices in Century City. Chef Mate did come through for us. Two waitstaff have been dispatched and are on their way. We are using the company's kitchen on the fourth floor and overflowing into the conference rooms.

I send Georgina in ahead of me, like a scout on a reconnaissance mission, to make sure the coast is clear and we can put this party together in the makeshift kitchen. The party is being hosted on the sixth floor in an area they call the ballroom. It is just a series of large rooms with sliding walls that open the space up to the next room. The larger the party, the more walls that go sliding. We are using three of the rooms so now it looks like one large room. The rental company dropped everything off earlier.

High cocktail tables are scattered in small rounds about the room. Beside them, tablecloths, napkins, glasses, plates, and cutlery sit in boxes waiting to transform the space.

The technical crew I'd booked to come in is here, using fishing line to hang a banner from the ceiling that reads like a newspaper headline, *Wynn Zimmerman Wins Again!* I get them busy hanging the evening's food and cocktail menus over the buffet tables when they are done. The menus are superimposed over newspaper articles promoting Wynn Zimmerman's clients.

I hear the elevator ring and the door opens to present Georgina, her excitement and awe with the way the room is coming together apparent.

"It's so much more fun to do these events when the client orders the décor too. It makes life worth living."

She directs a small staff to help decorate the rest of the room. They drape silk-screened tablecloths over the cocktail tables and arrange silverware. The bar is set up in the corner. My waitstaff and bartender arrive next, some of whom I'd used at the barbecue, and who have the look for this affair. I'd even arranged for a cigarette girl to wear rich red velvet and carry a box of cigar and cigarette choices. Everyone's waitstaff uniforms are in an office upstairs.

We set up three stations. Cold, hot, wet. The wet station, aka the bar, is out with the crowd. The cold and hot stations are inside our kitchen. Georgina commandeers the staff there to bake the hot hors d'oeuvres in perfectly timed intervals, and to arrange the cold hors d'oeuvres precisely as I'd directed her to earlier. We are ready for everything.

The bartenders get hit first, as the crowd starts to fill in, finding their rhythm with the thirsty crowd, dancing the glasses between them. To give the servers an air of times past, I had them dressed in sepia-toned vests and white shirts. They make rounds from the kitchen to the crowd and back again, expertly weaving their way around to get to everyone. The shrimp cocktail shots are a hot item, chilled, and easy to assemble quickly. They are set on a bed of crushed ice on top of a cocktail table in the center of the room. The elevator button rings all night as we move between floors, replenishing trays.

I watch the guests in action. Men making moves on the women, women making some moves on men, or at least throwing signals. I watch the guys with wedding rings inch closer to the short-skirted girls, their laughter rising and floating with the smoke. I wonder what the wives are doing now. Making themselves a lonely dinner or getting ahead in their own way. I hear back and forth promotional banter about how to handle a campaign, a cacophony of voices. Black dresses and nylons, loosened ties, and crocodile leather shoes. Cigarette smoke wafts to the ceiling. The cigarette girl rakes in tips. Glasses clink as they pass between guests. My servers are serving with a proficiency an expeditor would be proud of. And we all look good doing it.

Or at least Steve thinks so. He's been watching me, and my staff, in action. He was the one I was nervous about when I got the Wynn Zimmerman call in the first place, and sure enough he is here. Steve is magnetic. He wants to draw me toward the elevators. My conscience doesn't feel good about it at all. I can't say much about the rest of me. I definitely feel the pull. While I find the idea of an elevator experience enticing, I can't ever compromise my professional reputation by slowing down my waitstaff intentionally. If we hit the stop button in the elevator, the tray passes would be halted immediately. Guests would go thirsty, hungry even. And I know Steve doesn't have the clout to okay this and get away with it. I think sex between floors is a little too cliché anyway. We choose the office at the far end of the fourth floor instead where my staff had changed, as far away from the kitchen as possible. Believe me, it's better to get caught by your staff than caught by your client. The moral of that story is a long one. My morality is definitely in question.

There is a charge to the vibe in the ballroom when I return from my inter-office conference with Steve. The servers swerve around guests, offering our nibbles.

"Come back with more of those potato things," I hear while passing a small group of up-and-coming ad men.

I want to get back into the kitchen and see how my staff is doing. The scullery crew is busy washing platters and setting things back in place. Carlos's cousins are hard at work humming right along, talking and laughing, but never stopping. Georgina gathers some leftovers for Philip. The party is a huge success, and everyone finally leaves. Some happy. Some guilty. I go home with a dose of remorse because I'd mixed work with pleasure.

*!!***!!***!!*

STEVE CALLS me the next day and the next day, and the next day after that. I was doing my best to avoid him, but he just keeps calling and he wears me down. I agree to meet with him for a drink down the street, close to my house, so it won't be too inconvenient. We end up in my shabby chic living room where he quickly makes the moves on me, my Laura Ashley drapes still open. He blurts out, without warning, without even any sneaking suspicion on my part, that he's married.

"When," I ask, hoping he means he was married in the past.

I confuse him, but it doesn't stop him from wrestling with my pants. I can see the water in my flower vase swishing back and forth as our weight shifts determinedly. In no time he has his face between my legs and I am so excited at the idea of being caught in the cunning act of cunnilingus that I come instantly, surprising myself and his mouth. I stop, shuddering. I need to catch my breath. Stop what I was doing with him. He probably thinks I'm sexually repressed. Rather I'm sexually depressed. He asks if I want him to make me come again.

"No, thank you," I reply sullenly, the first time on record I have ever refused oral sex.

I dress myself—the ultimate tease. He thinks I'm kidding but I just can't go through with it. I decide not to sleep with him unless we are able to sleep together—as in really sleep, not just tumble around together pulling the sheets every which way. How many married men could manage a sleepover? I send him on his way. I have visions of his unsuspecting wife sitting at home watching the clock and waiting for him, his dinner cold and uneaten. I like her more than I like him at the moment. We'd probably be friends if given the chance. And if she wasn't happy with him, I probably wouldn't be happy either. Anyway, why reheat someone else's leftovers?

*!!***!!***!!*

THE FACT is, my father had many affairs when he was married to my mother. I was a child then, and although I didn't understand what an affair was, my mother's distrust of my father transferred from her consciousness to my subconscious and so the complication of intimacy followed.

I understood the icy glances over our Chef Express dinner plates then. I still enter every relationship with skepticism born from the past. The fact that my mother and father were not suited for each other certainly played a huge part in his infidelities. Poor Mother sitting at home on Saturday afternoons wondering whether he was telling the truth when he said he was going to the office to work or to the tennis court for a game of singles. It was the day she'd found his tennis racket in the basement that things took a catalytic turn for the worse. I wanted to close my eyes to the betrayal, but I was quietly relieved he'd finally found his freedom.

# Chapter Seven

## Chang/Ramirez Wedding

Menu for 350

Avocado & Sticky Rice Spring Rolls with Basil Leaves & Spicy Mango Dipping Sauce

Napa Cabbage Salad with Snap Peas, Bean Sprouts, Tangerine Sections & Sesame Seeds Tossed with Soy Vinaigrette

Braised Beef in Honey Garlic Sauce

Chicken Teriyaki, Soba Noodles in Secret Satay Sauce

Rapini & Bok Choy with Oyster Sauce

The phone rings. Simon says, "I'd like to come over."

*Hey, who am I to refuse?* He picks me up so we can go to Venice for dinner and then we spend another night in wanton self-abandon.

"Do you like that?" he asks later.

"Yeah, I like that. Keep doing it. Don't stop."

The next morning, we eat breakfast at my small dining table with the curtains open and the soft morning light hitting the table. He is playful. He's slabbing butter onto his bread in an exaggerated gesture while I look for my muffin tins. We've decided to bake eggs in a nest of spinach and goat cheese with toast on the side. We each have our tasks. While I add some chutney to the eggs, I see him pop his buttered bread into my toaster. Then he smears it with more butter when he pulls it out. He's living on the edge allowing butter to melt in my toaster. I tease him about it. He looks at me and shrugs, undaunted by my reprieve.

"I'm a ketchup with french fries kind of guy too. You should know that. Fries are nothing without ketchup. They'll go uneaten if there isn't any on hand."

"I'm learning."

We'd had enough meals together to know.

"No baked potato without the sour cream," he says. "No broccoli without the cheese sauce."

"I'm beginning to wonder how old you really are. Have I been fooled? Your eating habits are immature."

"I just enjoy life with all its toppings."

*!!***!!***!!*

"LIP SERVICE, may I help you?"

"Hi, it's me," he says.

I was trying to place *me*. I'd have to go along with him. "How's your day going?" I ask.

"It's going."

"Good."

"It'd be better if you were here."

I wondered where *here* is. *Whoever he is, he's relaxed enough to think there might only be one him. Which of them is the most self-assured?* My mind clicks and clanks, trying to figure it out. Good to know he is comfortable.

*Robert.* Ah ha.

"I'm back in town. How about dinner one night this week?"

"I'd love to have dinner with you, Robert."

"Well, great. How's Friday night?"

"Friday night would be perfect."

"Why don't I pick you up at eight?"

"Sounds good. I'll be ready."

I canceled my date with Simon.

"Is it because I let butter melt in your toaster?"

"No. Don't be silly."

"So I'm on my own for the night?"

"Yeah, this time around."

It's the day for my massage. Lil, my regular massage therapist, comes to my house with her table every other week on Friday, like clockwork. It's my time to unwind, erase the latent signs of work stress, and put the length back in my neck. Besides, I have Robert to get ready for.

"And what of love," I say to Lil, as she works on me. "Tell me. You're married. I want to know your side of the story." I need to know.

"I finish wiss the mans. There's no fooling around for me."

"Not even with your husband?"

She slaps me a little bit. She knows she can. "Oh, sure, of course with my husband. For me, there is only one mans," she quips. As if that's all I wanted to know.

"So love is monogamous for you then. It's not a free-for-all."

"Well, I'm no teenager. Sure."

"All right, so tell me how you fell in love. I really do want to hear your love story. I want to know how and when you fell in love."

"It was no miracle. He did all the things right. The things I needed at the time. Oh, yeah. We dated for months before everything else happened. He called. He showed up. We had nice times together. And one day I knew. He was there for me and I could fall in love."

"Are you still in love?"

"Yes and no. He is my man. That is it."

I relax into the massage, letting this sink in. Her strong, knowing hands dig into my muscles and tissue. I don't know if I am capable of her version of love—my recent activities a testimony to my doubts. I just can't seem to stop myself. I want the attention.

"You are seeing someone, yes?" she asks.

"Seeing yes. In love with no."

I begin to question my idea of commitment. The uncommitted part. The attachment to unattachment. Simon has it. I have it. We never speak of what a future might be for us. We sense the danger in it. It's a mutually gratifying exchange neither of us question. We fell quickly into lust and aren't prepared to give up sex so good in favor of the simple truth before us. Although I did love him in my own way. We share nothing but our appreciation for food, eroticism, and all the tempting desserts we can handle.

I tell myself this now. This is me. This is the best I can do. I can hope and pray all I want, but I'm only me. In the far reaches of my mind I am afraid of many things. I am afraid of myself and what I might do. I am afraid Simon will find out about Robert. I am afraid Robert will find out about Simon. They are each my ace in the hole, my backup plan. I doubt sex so good with Simon would last. I don't know Robert enough to even guess where this is going.

I take a hot bath with Epsom salts making the most of my massage and soak for a really long time. I am refreshed, relaxed, and relatively romantic when Robert shows up.

"Hi, Gwen." He kisses me on the cheek, a quick hello that doesn't linger. "I thought we'd drive along Sunset Boulevard to the Palisades and have dinner. My cousin is performing in a play there. I have tickets. It would be good I think."

He lets me know at dinner that his parents would be at the theatre. The fact that he'd be introducing me to them seems a good sign. I am nervously excited. He kisses me over dinner and holds my hand while toasting.

"Well, here's to us and new beginnings."

I am guarded but play along. I am navigating new territory and have my wits about me.

"What do your parents do?" I ask, probing innocently.

"They're retired. Dad worked for Boeing. Mom was a stay-at-home mom. He retired twelve years ago. She retired when we moved out."

"Do mothers ever retire?"

"I guess not. She still cooks for me. But now I have you. Which makes me want to know when you might cook for me?"

"Well, it won't be this week. I have a wedding to cater for a very demanding client. I plan on eating standing up until it's over."

"So you're going to let me starve then?"

"Well, there is your mom."

*!!***!!***!!*

HER WEDDING is being held at the Manor, at the edge of the foothills above Pasadena. I meet my client, Consuela Ramirez, there to do a walk-through of the location and to go over the schedule. She insists her entire Latino family will be all right with the Asian menu her fiancé's family wants. I offer to do some Mexican appetizers at least, but she won't hear of it.

"Just make sure there's enough ice cold Pacifico, lots of lime, and perfect margaritas all night long. The mariachi band is hired already."

Consuela is icy cold herself and I imagine Thom Chang, her fiancé, might be as well, but when I finally meet him he is quite the opposite. He seems in quiet awe of his Consuela. She has free rein to throw her weight around making these arrangements, and from what I can tell, she has his blessing. They came in together so we can discuss the tea ceremony. A moment, he tries to relate, that is steeped in ritual and one whose importance cannot be overlooked.

Mariachi band notwithstanding, the food is somehow irrelevant to him. He is poised. Soft spoken. He is paying for everything. The fact that I don't understand their union won't interfere with my ability to pull it together for them. Their date is looming closer and I've started preparations. Even Nadine, the best food rep this side of the Pacific, can't help me with all the ingredients for my Asian Flare menu, so I know a trip downtown to Chinatown is imminent.

"The sauce, the sauce. The secret is in the sauce." I purr to Georgina. "Let's make a list. Let's make it complete, so I don't have to make two trips like the last time I did this menu. Rice paper, chili sauce, toasted sesame seeds, rice vinegar, soba noodles, oyster sauce. Soy sauce."

"Check," she says, "what else?"

"Ginger, garlic, honey. Red and green peppers."

"Check, check, check. Check, check."

"Lemon grass."

"You put lemon grass in your teriyaki sauce?"

"That's the secret."

"Hey, what should I put down for the satay sauce?" she asks. Georgina's so on top of things, she knows I've skipped the secret satay sauce ingredients.

"It's another secret. Why would I tell you that? The lemon grass in teriyaki sauce is enough of a secret for one day. Let me worry about the satay sauce."

The phone rings to reveal Robert on the line. I kick the door to my office closed so Georgina doesn't hear me. The lip phone is pressed to my own lips.

"I simply can't live without you. I miss you desperately," he claims.

"As if."

"No, really. I must see you."

"Well, I'm just about to go to Chinatown."

"How exotic. Don't mind if I do."

Robert wants to come along? Shopping? With me?

"Really?" I say. I can hear the incredulous quality in my voice. As if he's asked for something more complicated. I hope he doesn't think I'm so surprised he guesses I'm socially deprived. Because I'm not really. I'm just not used to tagalongs with a man. Shopping is a personal affair I've grown accustomed to doing alone.

"I think I should supervise. Let's have lunch down there," he suggests.

It's a nice afternoon. We eat a late lunch in a quiet restaurant, where the servers dote on us. We laugh and question each other about where we've been and where we want to go. Not only in the world, but in a relationship too. He's investigative. He seems to like exploring the what-ifs. *What if I decide right now you're perfect for me, and this lunch never ends?*

He helps me unload everything into the kitchen when we return.

"Well, when am I going to see you again?"

"Ooh, that's a tough one with the wedding and all."

"Don't make me crash it. I'll call you tomorrow and we'll go from there."

I want to keep Robert at arm's length, but I am highly unskilled at it and I didn't expect such persistence on his part. His goodbye kiss is light, his hug like a bear hug.

*!!***!!***!!*

THERE ARE phone calls during the day to plan our next night together. I let him take the lead. I don't put much effort into getting this off the ground, but I am receptive and obliging when he makes the effort. I'm reassuring. He's confident.

"I'm coming to you tonight. I'm cooking," he says.

"Really?"

"Really. It will be the best meal you've ever had."

"See you soon."

He comes over late Thursday night with a large pizza and a six-pack of Sam Adams.

"That's your idea of cooking?" I ask when I see the pizza box.

"Hell, yes, I had to buy a pizza oven to make this work," he jokes. He pops a couple tops while I plate a few slices and we munch happily, dreamily. He produces a pack of cigarettes after dinner. It's the first time I've seen him with them. He's never even mentioned he smokes.

"Tell me, Gwen, where do you see us in five years? Where are we living? What cars do we drive? Are you still working or are you going to let me support our happy lifestyle? Where do we vacation?"

"I don't know where to begin."

"Let's start by getting close. I mean really close. Let's tell each other everything. Go ahead, you start. What do you hope for? What do you dream about?"

"Wow, you're grilling me like a cheese sandwich."

"I want to share everything with you."

"You do?"

"Yes. Even the cheese sandwich. And what's great is that our love will grow as we grow to know each other and even if we're challenged, we'll have each other to lean on."

He sucks a long drag out of his cigarette and then gives me a raunchy, smoky kiss.

"It's suspicious," he says, "we're good. Even with pizza, beer, and cigarette breath, we're good."

We have sex all night. There is no stopping him. It is so hard and so fast my innie nearly becomes an outie. By the time he leaves, there are belongings strewn about the living room. Each pile of clothing, each crumpled blanket a sensual memory.

We have coffee the next morning and I leave his cup on my honey maple dining table, removing all the other dirty dishes except that one cup. I want to leave it there like a shrine. Proof that something has happened.

*!!***!!***!!*

SIMON SAYS, "Have you forgotten about me?"

*!!***!!***!!*

THERE ARE many nights with Robert. They overflow, one into the other. He has a toothbrush in my bathroom. He gets dressed for work in the morning at my house. He's even brought his favorite coffee to add to my pantry. After a quickie one morning he takes a rushed shower and hurries out the door, planting a deep kiss on my lips.

"See ya soon. Call ya sooner," he says, and is gone.

I'm pretty much sold. He loves me—although he hasn't said so exactly—I believe he does. He wants me, I tell myself. *Da, how long have you been wanting that.* My reasoning mind kicks in when I am alone without him. Before I know it, I'm reaching for pen and paper and making a pros and cons list. Pro. He likes me, wants me. Con. He likes me, wants me. Pro. He's age appropriate, emotionally available, and geographically desirable. Con. He's age appropriate, emotionally available, geographically desirable. You get the idea. I am in trouble. I'm sure of it. I've grown so accustomed to being alone, all this is frightening. I can taste the fear in my mouth, like the tinny taste of bile rising from my stomach.

I decide it's time to see Simon, hoping I'll find him hopelessly attractive and Robert less so. Seeing Simon has a completely unexpected outcome. I'm really happy to see him, our dinner is fun, and I fall for the tricks up Simon's sleeve, and yet I miss Robert immensely. The longing I have for him is real. It eats through me like the holes in swiss cheese, leaving me exposed and empty. I am sure Simon must be able to tell my attention is divided. Maybe I can love two men at once. I muse and rationalize.

Simon is asleep beside me now and the ceiling is on top of me, closing in. I'll be waking up with Simon in the morning. He'll be buttering his bread before he puts it into my toaster. I resign myself to this reality. It's only society that dictates I can love only one at a time. Who am I to act with discernment?

I see Simon on Friday night. Robert's out of town again so I think I can get away with it. I begin to use Simon as a bridge to bide my time without Robert. I start lying in subtle ways. At first, I barely even notice, but soon enough I'm having to backtrack through the corridors of my mind, trying to remember what I'd told Simon about my week. What I'd done, what I'd not done. Maybe I've just set my own trap.

"Are you hungry?" I ask.

"Not particularly," he replies.

"So why are you eating?"

"Because it's dinner time. I always eat when it's dinner."

"Are you going to eat dessert too?"

"Probably. I always eat a little dessert. Why do you ask?"

"No reason."

He is becoming predictable—or has he been all along and I am finally noticing it?

*!!***!!***!!*

I'm such a chicken, I think with a twisted smirk as I pull the nearly thawed chicken breasts apart from each other and give Georgina the teriyaki sauce ingredients. "I'm surprised you're not using a store brand sauce."

"I'm surprised you're surprised. Me? Store brand sauce?" A cheater sauce as I call it. Who does she think I am? Cheater, cheater, pumpkin eater. Given my current reality with Simon & Robert, I second guess myself momentarily. The moment is gone as quickly as my guilt.

The Ramirez wedding is fewer than three days away now. All the elements are in place. I thank God Consuela is confident enough in my abilities to stay out of my way and let me do my job. The only issue I have with her is her insistence on using only chopsticks. There are just too many people of non-Asian persuasion to let this happen. My food would not shine if guests are chopstick impaired.

"But it's an Asian menu," Consuela implores, the day we discuss eating utensils.

Trying to make my clients feel like they've won a concession even when they haven't, is an art I perfected long ago. You just have to take charge of the moment, fill their heads with everything positive that's in good working order as it relates to their event, and then go in for the kill.

"Yes, of course there are going to be chopsticks on the table. And the forks and knives will be at a side table ready when needed." Notice there are no buts or howevers anywhere in that statement. Notice it's a statement, not a question. I don't give Consuela any room for debate.

*!!***!!***!!*

We're sharing a pizza I made from scratch with all the little ingredients Georgina readied earlier. Artichoke hearts, arugula, sun-dried tomato, smoked gouda, and buffalo mozzarella, grilled zucchini. My desk is a table, too, when we need it to be.

"Let's go over logistics, Georgina. We have one hour to turn the ceremony room into a stunning reception hall, and we have to do it quietly, quickly. Our newly married couple and all their guests will be upstairs going through the receiving line while we work downstairs. So let's get tables with locking wheels so we can roll everything in—already dressed and set. We can be doing that behind closed doors during the reception."

I called a new girl in to help with prep. She shows up wearing Birkenstocks and a worn T-shirt—no bra. Her ample breasts jiggle as she introduces herself as Katie. I give her instructions and run for the phone as it rings and rings. I can see her getting touchy-feely with some of the ingredients while I talk on the phone. Squeezing tangerines. Massaging the avocados. Touching her hair and then the mangoes. I am getting so nervous watching her. I don't like having her in my kitchen. I put my hand over the phone.

"Georgina, did you see that? Can you see what she's doing? She can't touch herself that way. Not here. She needs to put her hair back."

I concentrate on the secret satay sauce. It's simple really—after I grind my own Spanish peanuts, I add the soy sauce and tamarind, the dark brown sugar, all my other secret ingredients, and coconut milk. Katie's watching me like a hawk. I swear she's a spy from one of my competitors. She comes closer and as she's reaching toward me, she says, "Can I try it? Is it done? It looks good."

I'm afraid she'll dip her finger in the bowl to try it. I pull it away impulsively, well out of her reach.

"Georgina, why don't you have Katie start peeling and dicing mangoes for the mango sauce?"

"Oh, I love mangoes. I'm good at cutting them to avoid the pit."

"Well, then, you're perfect for the job. Great."

She pulverizes the mangoes. She makes dice look like a massacre. Everything she touches turns sticky. With my luck I'll be the first person to pick up something she just had her hands on and get the stickiness on me. It gives me shivers.

"I have a confession to make," she says later.

I look up from my cutting board.

"I don't wash my iceberg lettuce," she claims.

"Who does? You'll wash my Napa cabbage though, won't you?"

She won't be returning tomorrow.

*!!***!!***!!*

I'M TOO busy to even see Robert when he returns from his business trip, but he convinces me to join him for a nightcap after my longest day that week. I really need a good night's sleep, but what I get is a good night's *bleep*. Nonetheless, all of this sidetracking is getting to me. It is hard to stay focused on my work—as much as I want a relationship, I don't know how to do both.

*!!***!!***!!*

SIMON SAYS, "Call me back. I never see you anymore."

I can't very well say I am so exhausted because I was up until five A.M., doing the nasty with my new favorite lover. Well, maybe I can, but that might upset the delicate balance of my relationship with Simon.

I wonder what Robert might think if he knows I want to have my cake and share it too.

*!!***!!***!!*

THEIR CEREMONY is taking place on the rolling lawns. They stand together in an open gazebo with the priest, while my staff bustles behind the scenes. I'm still having a hard time seeing this odd couple together. I soften my focus, dreamily—and suddenly it's not Consuela I see or her husband in waiting. It's me. *Oh, and look*—if I squint just right—there's Robert waiting for me to walk up the aisle, pulling at his shirt collar.

*Well, then, that's it.* I decide. I will let Robert in. I will let him be my man. I will let him lead the way and that will be that. We'll marry. We'll live happily ever after. He's already hinted at it. I'm confident everything is fine.

We're ready to go. The first hour we serve 150 people with avocado sticky rice spring rolls and spicy mango dipping sauce.

"What's that?" Consuela's cousin Chi Chi asks, when I push the platter in her face.

"They're spring rolls."

"But they're not fried."

"Try one. They're delicious."

"I don't know."

"Really, they're good. They're just like an enchilada, but instead of cheese and tortilla they're made with rice paper and vegetables. Try one with the dipping sauce."

Between seven and nine P.M., the crowd grows to 350. Plates are stacked on tables behind silk screens. My staff is arranging salads and the servers are ready to fly them into the round banquet tables set up around the room.

There are toasts and speeches and tears between each course of our menu, as we plate, serve, collect, plate and serve again, and again.

*!!***!!***!!*

THE CHINESE tea ceremony is a ritual-like exchange. We set up the teacups and smaller sniffing cups on each table prior to dinner. Thom hired the tea master, now busy boiling spring water in several glass pots he set up on portable gas burners in our kitchen area. The tea master is a serious man and moves with quiet deliberation, using long pointed chopsticks to add buds of tea to the individual teapots.

Young women in silk sarongs silently deliver the red clay sand teapots to each of the tables. They return with the boiling water in clear carafes and pour it into the pots, letting the tea steep for barely a minute. The pungent fragrance of lilac and honeysuckle fills the room when they pour the tea, not into each cup separately, but in a back and forth motion that fills all the cups at the same time. They step back from the tables at the same time, their movements synchronized.

The guests drink the tea in unison and return the cups to the middle of the table. The ritual is repeated over and over four more times with as much ceremony as the first time. It was gracious and peaceful, quiet and moving.

Then the mariachi band starts to play. Loudly. So loud, the groom's father approaches me to ask them to tone it down a notch. It is hard for me to even get their attention, but I manage. Minutes later, Consuela's cousin Chi Chi is telling them to up the volume, shaking her ample hips and giving them the thumbs up. She knows them all. They are listening to her. It is a tug of war back and forth, loud and soft.

By the time we're wrapping up in the kitchen it's time to cut the cake. Thom and Consuela's hands join at the bottom layer of the multitiered masterpiece and the room grows quiet as they slice a piece. Then they cut it in two. Each holds a piece of it in their hands, with arms intertwining. They feed it to each other. I want some of that—the cake, the ceremony to go with it, the beginning of a life together—the icing on the cake.

The loud mariachi band is long forgotten. They are asleep on the grass outside. Their hats are tossed aside, and turned upside down.

*!!***!!***!!*

I PULL into my driveway and barely put the top up on my convertible when Robert calls me on my cell phone. He invites me by to see his house. Maybe it is a sign. He is calling. The voice through the phone like a beacon, beckoning.

It is the moment I've been waiting for and it is upon me. He is waiting for me. His head peeks out from the doorway of his bedroom as I enter his house. I've never been here. I am inside his inner sanctum. He disappears from the doorway and when next I see him, he is in bed, his hair falling against the pillow like strands of stuck-together spaghetti. You might think I rushed to his home at that late hour to let him enter me and that's my sole motivation. But it is the curiosity that drove me there. It was my soul calling. I still hadn't made up my mind what was best by the time I realize I am trapped in my clothes.

Claustrophobic suddenly, I rip at my sweater to release its clutch around me. I want to be free and unencumbered. Newly naked and nakedly nude. Clothes off, my hands are reaching for his flesh—silky skin reminds me of coconut milk and the beads around his neck add a texture of sandalwood I am drowning in. I let him do what he wants to do with me. Asking me to come, wanting to watch me before he releases himself into me. Receptive and open, I surrender to him and his desire to fill my needs. Sweet orgasmic pleasures. It's the pillow talk time that makes me warm and tingly inside. Lying there beside him, arms wrapped in a cacophony of directionless limbs, bed linens twisted around us.

"I like you, Gwen."

"I like you, too, Robert."

"I like you in my bed."

I play with his ear. It is soft and smooth. I lie listening to the sound of his quiet breath and let the night slip away around me. I want to preserve this moment like a jar of jam, sealed forever in my mushy mind and gushy heart.

# Chapter Eight

## Van Buren Bachelorette Party

Hot & Cold Hors d'Oeuvres Menu for 20
Mini Caramelized Onion & Brie Quesadillas with Chipotle & Roasted Corn Salsa
Polenta Rounds with Roasted Red Pepper Coulis
Cheese Plate with Champagne Grapes & Figs
Wine Bar

I'm sipping on a new cabernet, bedside, with food porn all over my mattress, *Gourmet*, *Gourmand*, *Bon Appétit*, splayed vulnerably across the sheets. I'm salivating over the pictures and ingredients. It's about as much fun as I can have with my pjs on. My phone rings out of nowhere, pulls me out of pure bliss.

"Hi, Gwen, so I have a favor to ask." It's Genevieve.

"I'm listening." But really, I'm still salivating.

"Dan invited me to Catalina—he wants to sail there, he has a nice boat, actually, and well—."

"You're still seeing each other? That's great."

"I was reluctant to tell you much in case you were hurt, or jealous. I didn't know if I liked him all that much, but he was so sweet at your dinner party, and I figured if you weren't into him—."

"Of course, sure. Trust me, I have enough on my plate already."

"Yeah, so I wanted to ask if you'd take care of my bird, Hermie, while we're gone. I'll bring the cage, and the food, and the little blanket to make his world night."

"Does he like night during the day?"

"Well, no, not every day, but when he falls asleep, I put the blanket over his cage. If the trip goes well, we'll be gone for weeks. He's easy. He does sing a bit. I'll be in touch."

I'm thinking he's going to party all night and sleep during the day. I think our schedules are off already. I'm a little skeptical when she appears the next morning with the cage. Hermie's along for the ride, and so am I.

"I've never taken care of a bird before."

Genevieve plops the cage on the end table closest to my front window, right beside my couch. There is a blanket, long enough to cover him up but she's still holding it. We're all watching the neighborhood at the same time.

"He's a good bird, Gwen."

"Well, I think Dan's a good egg, Genevieve. Have a great time."

This unexpected responsibility has given me pause to ponder. I need a break after Consuela's wedding anyway. I open the door of his cage and stick my finger in. He hops onto it, his yellow head and orange spotted cheeks bobbing his thanks.

He waddles up my hand, across my wrist, and along my arm, my fingers protruding, and he climbs onto my index finger. I place him on top of his cage, hoping he'll hop inside, where he can climb a ladder or swing on a swing, miniature to match his small bird size.

I do the dishes in the sink. I hear Hermie's wings flutter above the sounds of the Chopin I'm listening to and the water running from the kitchen tap. Suddenly he is on my head, a swooped landing that gets louder as he nears my ears. My hands are wet and soapy, so I let him stay on my head.

He walks across the terrain of my freshly washed and dried hair, and I hope he won't poop while he's visiting. It's an odd sensation to have a bird's claw-like feet come up against my scalp. A scratchy kind of probe. When I finish the dishes, I walk to his cage. He's still on my head, his claws bracing against the movement. I reach up, extend my hand, an invitation for him to climb aboard. I put him back on top of his cage, hoping he'll leave me alone for a while.

I make tea. Ceremoniously. Part of me is still steeped in the beauty of the tea ceremony at the Ramirez wedding. Jasmine tea. Aromatic even after the milk is added. I search the cupboard for some Scottish biscuits. Hermie's watching me. And so goes the day.

By the time I sit at my café-style table to pour the tea from the pot into the cup and reach for a biscuit, he's flown over again, using my head as a landing strip. I pull him onto my hand and he leaps onto the table. He's no fool. He sees the biscuits and inches toward them. A lot of personality is packed into his tiny body. I let him get really close to the cookies before I move them out of the way making a clucking sound. I hope he understands. Bird-talk for scram. He follows after them and I admire his persistence. I let this go on for a while, and then I reach for him and put him back in his cage. Or at least try to.

Up he hops right onto the top of it, looking over his shoulder, trying to avoid my groping hand—like a cat-and-mouse game. Then he hops up onto my finger and lets me ease him into his metal jungle. Eventually he twists his neck around and sticks his beak into his back and closes his eyes. I put his blanket over his cage hoping not to wake him, and I go to bed thinking all is fine in my world.

I wake up feeling a sense of purity and splendor—fresh linens on my bed kind of purity. I lie there feeling the weight of the sheets against my skin, hearing the sounds of morning outside my window. I feel exuberant.

I can hear the phone ringing in the living room and then Robert's voice on the answering machine.

By the time I get from my bedroom, through the hallway, and into my kitchen I am overwhelmed. All this time I've been thinking I want a relationship and have been whining to my friends about how unsuitable every man has been. Now that I've managed to get one, I'm getting cagey. Just like Hermie.

I pull the blanket off his cage so he can see the day. I am tempted to let him free. I opt for somewhat free and open the door of his cage. Not just so he can fly around the house, but free, free, out into the world of trees that could be his playground. I can't stand the idea of us both suffering.

Robert's voice is filling the room, but I can't pick up. I'm immobilized. Hermie flies clear across the room and lands on top of my drapery rod. He's got a bird's-eye of the room and my sudden paralysis. A vast open desert plain wouldn't be big enough to separate Robert and me sufficiently for me to feel safe again. The uncharted territory of my emotional psyche, all the places I haven't been able to go to because I've not had a worthy partner, is now stripped open and lies bare before me. *Eek. Eek. Double eek.*

I am reminded of my three engagements, all broken by yours truly because I thought I'd be miserable. Okay, in my defense, maybe they were wrong for me in the long run. It's sad that I'm waiting for the shoe to drop. I ask myself constantly why can't I just trust and believe that this is good, that this is right, but my doom-and-gloom mentality is keeping itself honed on the short end of the wishbone. It'll never work. I am sure of it. He'll do something wrong and disappoint me, or I won't be enough for him somehow.

Before I know it, I'm a manic mess.

In a twisted effort to calm myself, I contemplate calling Patricia, a friend I don't speak with often because she's married and—let's face it—I'm not. She's always been so pro-marriage. I think maybe she has some good advice for me.

I learned through Genevieve, though, that Patricia's husband just left her for another woman, leaving her with the children and the bills for their matrimonial home on the hill. This is a man she is in love with. Just last week she was telling me how great their sex was and this week he is gone—*hasta la vista* baby. I finally materialize an age appropriate, geographically desirable, single, looking to be married kind of man, and instead of running with it I want to run from it. So intent on sidestepping my own innate ability to advise myself, I am reaching for the phone and have dialed nine out of Patricia's ten numbers before I stop myself and put the phone down.

I spend a few minutes reasoning with myself and try to exercise at least a little self-control. First, I think it would be self-centered and insensitive to call Patricia for advice. Ill-advised, as well, since any advice is going to be clouded through her recent faithlessness in the sacrament of marriage. I decide I'm better off talking to myself in the mirror. This self-talk is less costly for one thing, than the long distance, and I think I'm more apt to trust my own advice over Patricia's. It's possible I won't talk to Patricia for months, maybe years. She'll be elbow deep in divorce and custody proceedings, and I think I'll be in love for a while. I'm assuming Robert and I will figure out some way to make it work.

I'll call her when I'm on a downswing—when we both have something to complain about. That way our friendship will deepen. I feel better. I let Hermie land on my finger and put him back in his cage. He seems happy to be in it, and I am immediately at ease.

*Ooh.* Still. Maybe I don't want a marriage. *Maybe I just want an arrangement. Maybe Simon and I are fine after all.*

As it turned out, I didn't have to call Patricia. She called me. I didn't have to worry about telling her about the new man, the hopeful man, the man who would change my life if I let him man. Man, oh man, could she talk. I tried slipping in a tidbit of information about the goings on in my life but that didn't work. She was turning cynically critical and I got scared into silence. She'd turned bittersweet without the sweet. She was a hopeless romantic without the romantic and I was a hopeful man lover with a man. No wonder love is blind. If it weren't, no one would commit. I'll bet Patricia didn't see it coming. What didn't I see? I wondered.

*!!***!!***!!*

ASIDE FROM Patricia's misfortune, there are relationships brewing all around me as my double life ensues. Everything feels like spring. Dan and Genevieve are already traveling together. Georgina and Philip are tagging the nine-month mark and a ring is imminent. They're getting closer to a wedding date. Love is all around me. I will soon join the ranks of coupledom. I can feel it in my bones. The dating foreplay is over. I want Robert and it seems he wants me. He has made signs he wants to become more serious, so it's best I clear the decks anyway.

I am beginning to feel a sense of loyalty to him. That was fast. We stop for dessert one night and a drop-dead gorgeous hunk of man with intense eyes is at the counter waiting to serve us. As Robert is deciding on what dessert to order for us, I am giving the guy at the counter the eye. I can't believe myself. The eye that says *I'd love to do you, man, but this is the man I'm going home with tonight. Guess what we're going to do later?* I smile at him. *Who am I?* I'm such a bad girl. I don't know if there is hope for me.

*!!***!!***!!*

I HAVE to keep my wits about me. Shelly Van Buren's upcoming bachelorette party is a happy sidestep for me. I've grown to love her in my own way. From engagement party to bridal shower she's shown her loyalty. I understand her enough to give her and Adam what they want. I'll get to know her in a different way at the bachelorette party. We booked a suite at the Hollywood Roosevelt Hotel even though we knew we'd be sneaking the food and staff into it. A memorable venue however. The wedding is just around the corner. She entrusts me with the activities for the evening which include a mini casino setup with roulette wheel and blackjack table. If love is a gamble, maybe I prefer blackjack.

I have a few extra surprises up my sleeve, but Shelly won't know anything until that night. I let Allison in on my plans. She is tickled with my idea of booking a stripper for the party. "Do you know any strippers? Because I do," she says. "My best friend goes to Boom Boom in Long Beach. We could get someone from there. I hear they're all big hunks."

"It's not really my scene but that doesn't mean I don't know how to find one. Leave it to me. I've got it all figured out. There are services for these things."

*!!***!!***!!*

I THINK of Simon and me. To let something amount to nothing and for so long is wrong, I think. I am afraid I will sacrifice long-term compatibility with Robert for our short-term gratification. I'm doing myself a great disservice, but it is hard to pull away from my weekly dinner date with Simon and night of flesh-grabbing exploration. Although, the sex hasn't been that good lately. It lacks the emotional value we had in the beginning and I'm surprised it's come to this—full circle in such a short time.

It will be up to me to change this status. He's not going to end it. He's having a great time. I'm sure he thinks I'm easy to be with. No demands, no hassle, no problem.

I may be sad when it's over, but will I miss him or long for him? What am I giving up? I examine my motivation then for not wanting to end it and I realize it's dinner. It's the dressing up part and the being taken out part and the not being expected to pay part, and all those glorious dishes being placed in front of me part. It's not about him at all. I'm slightly ashamed at my own honesty.

I do not take myself out for dinner. I cook. I always have ingredients on hand to make something and I can almost guarantee the outcome of my own prepared entrées. I can satisfy my fickle taste more appropriately than a restaurant chef.

*!!***!!***!!*

IT TAKES me several more weeks before I end it with Simon.

Simon says, "Why say goodbye? Things are perfect. We're so compatible."

"But where's this going? Really. It's so casual. You seem content with the way things are, but I need more depth, something I can really sink my teeth into."

*‼***‼***‼*

I HAVE just enough time to have Lil massage me and get over to the Roosevelt. Georgina is ahead of me by an hour. She's made multiple trips up and down the service elevators with supplies, quietly, stealthily. She doesn't want to get caught.

The girls arrived one by one, semi dressed up, excited and giddy. The maid of honor and the ladies-in-waiting gathered in the foyer of the suite to talk brass tacks about Shelly's impending wedding. They are all good friends at ease with each other.

"All right. Now that that's out of the way, let the games begin," Allison exclaims.

Night has already fallen and the view from the suite offers scenes of LA's Friday night rush-hour traffic. There are horns blaring, sirens whirling, and the odd cacophony of voices down below. We put the wet bar to good use and the food is on end tables and the desk in the living room, all within easy reach of the sitting areas. There is just enough seating for all the girls.

At eleven P.M., I feign that we are out of red wine and make a mock call to Vic Turner's on Sunset to deliver some more. Scores of people know how reliable Vic Turner's is and he's open twenty-four seven.

"Hey, everybody, they'll be right here. There's more wine on the way."

Cheers from all the girls.

There is a rap at the door, and suddenly I am too busy to get it. The quesadillas are warming and they need my full attention.

"Allison, can you get the door please?" She is closest.

"What and turn my back on these cheating poker players?" She reaches for the door anyway. She directs the deliveryman to the bar area and sits right back down, resuming her hand. Talk about a poker face. Everyone else is oblivious to the treat in store.

"I'm winning this hand girls. I just am," Shelly says.

The deliveryman offers to open one of the bottles of red wine and pours a glass for our bride-to-be, Shelly. When I give him the high sign, he walks across the room and hands it to her.

"Oh, thank you," she oozes, sipping from the glass immediately.

Allison picks up her glass and proposes a toast. "Ladies, may I have your attention. Here's to Shelly and the exciting life she has ahead of her with Adam."

"Here, here."

"And here's to the exciting night she has ahead of her with Raul," I add.

"Here, here."

"Who's Raul?" she asks, suddenly attentive, eyeing the deliveryman.

"I am Raul," he replies, "and this is me."

With that he removes his shirt showing a physique we all wanted a piece of. He grabs a bunch of grapes, hangs them out of his pockets. He straddles Shelly lickety-split.

"Are you hungry, lady?"

*!!***!!***!!*

Sometimes you live your life and sometimes it lives you. Sometimes everything is perfectly fine in your heart and mind and you're so busy projecting your perfect fantasy world for your own enjoyment you don't even see reality.

Ask your man what he thinks of your relationship and see how surprised you'll be when he describes something completely different than what you'd describe. We hit a glitch—Robert and I. I overreacted to something he'd said, but I didn't see it at the time. I did see how I was setting myself up for failure, blowing this whole incident out of proportion though. A part of me really wants to talk about it to everyone I know except him, so that it becomes an epic drama that supersedes real life altogether and probably ends up in a theatre near me. I need to converse with him but I've already said things I shouldn't have.

I opt to call my voice mail number and listen to my saved messages. I know there're at least a few from him I have from when everything was grand. They were juicy messages. I press the numbers on the keypad and listen to the first, then the second. When I hear them all, I listen to them over again. My heart sinks like a soufflé pulled from the oven too soon. I listen to all the promises and know I can't walk away from the relationship.

I have to learn new tools to save myself from certain moral demise. I can't ruin this for the sake of ruining it—believing in some warped icky way that I don't deserve love and am not worthy of the happiness that love can bring.

The next day, he dumps me. Boy, do I have egg on my face. Here I've been living in my own fantasy world and I hadn't heard him hinting at the end all along. I thought I'd kept my ears open. He'd been saying goodbye long before he was gone.

So shocked was I to hear him say, "It's over, Gwen," that I still didn't believe it.

"But why?" I implore. "Just because we hit a glitch? So let's smooth it out."

"I don't want to."

"That's it? The first sign of trouble and you pack it in? Just like that?"

"I've been thinking about this for a while."

"Well, thanks for letting me know."

"I've been trying to tell you."

"Really? When? When I was between your legs the other night?"

"Don't be crude."

"Don't be vague."

No one's ever dumped me. I scan my memory for pain of this sort and see that no, I have not been dumped before. I always do the ending. What good is a fantasy world if you can't write your own ending?

I reach for the phone to call Georgina instead. I can't be alone with my own thoughts right now. "I thought maybe he was fooling around on me, but he was living a comfortable lie while falling out of love with me."

"I don't think it's over," she says, "he just put you on hold. Guys are like that. They think they can stop time, and when they're ready for you, they expect you'll be there."

I think, I'll move at lightning speed to get over him and have another man by the time he realizes what he's lost and is ready for another round of the love game. *Yeah right, Gwen,* I say to myself, not wanting to admit my real pain.

I listen to his messages again. Oh, his voice, how it pierces through me like the stabbing of the vegetables I'm spearing for my shish kebab dinner. A dinner I thought I'd be preparing for him. How can something so deep be removed so quickly. I just can't believe it's over.

I feel I've missed something. This is not reminiscent of the behavior I knew from boys when I was growing up. Why am I only learning this now? After all the men I've seen come and go and come again. I feel I am seeing this species for the first time. I check my premise and wonder if maybe the change started with me. I had expectations after all. Many of them. A whole loaf of them sliced and ready for the making. I had them in starting this business, too, but that hasn't been a problem. I am learning that a business is so much easier than a relationship. It's easier to be a singular entity working for a singular goal. The two-person endeavors are confusing. There's too much of the unknown at every step. Sure, you think you know someone—no someone is more like it.

There are five people in every relationship, I decide. No wonder I've been having trouble. Him, her, his idea of her, her idea of him, and them. Wait! There are two more. Her idea of herself and his idea of himself within the context of them. It's a wonder anyone even gets to the altar. And how do the ones that make it, make it last?

I finish preparing my dinner and let Hermie out of his cage. He flies here and there around my living room. I'm so happy to have his company. He flies up to the curtain rod above my living room window and sits there a moment. Then he leaps carelessly from his perch. Erratically he swoops from above and, like a wounded fighter pilot, plunges quickly to the floor, hitting it with his precious little head. And just like that he's dead.

No. No. No. I can't take it. Hermie was my friend. And I'd just watched him commit suicide. What would I tell Genevieve? I sink to the floor beside his lifeless body wracking sobs for the loss of my feathered friend. It's enough to send tears escaping for the loss of both Robert and Simon, and the loss of my innocence in trying to love. I'm crying for all that I am afraid to admit about myself. Crying for my cocky naïveté because I know I have to accept all these truths about myself. The only consolation is that Hermie is now free of this unkempt world. I am crying for all that I'd hoped for and still don't have.

*!!***!!***!!*

DAYS LATER, numb from my eyeballs down, as I'm trying to figure out what to say to Genevieve about Hermie's death dive, she calls. I don't want to pick up, but I have to.

"We're having such a good time we're going to keep sailing west. Can you keep Hermie until I get back?"

"Of course. Have a great time. I'm so happy you're happy." There's not much happy in my voice.

I can't say much else. I'm about to dive deeper into my instant depression when Robert calls and helps me take the plunge. He calls again and again. I decide not to return his phone calls. Why does he dump me and then call all the time? It's not fair to dangle a carrot and then eat it in front of me.

Finally, I answer, "Why are you calling me?"

"I feel badly for how things have turned out."

"So what do you want to do about it?"

"Well, nothing really. I just wanted to let you know you're not the only one who's hurting."

This is all bigger than I am and I am not in control. Just like I wasn't in control when Hermie flew to his death. I still wasn't sure what I'd tell Genevieve about that. His precious little body was preserved in my freezer in a Ziploc bag behind the ice cube trays.

Maybe I have to thank Robert for setting me free to find a more complete love. Perhaps. I don't know for sure. I am lost. I have forgotten what I'm preparing for tomorrow. I can't remember whether I ate before I showered or showered before I ate breakfast this morning.

*!!***!!***!!*

FOR DAYS phone calls pour in from the bachelorette party girls. Shelly and then Allison gush at how great a time they had. One of the girlfriends wants to inquire for future reference what my fees are for parties and how they might be able to use me.

*!!***!!***!!*

I'M WONDERING what to do with all this love that seems so real. What will I make of the batter once the dough is rolled out? I'm usually so good at knowing what is real and what is a lie. Maybe Robert's own lie is so convincing that he is sending off *this is real* vibes and fogging my vision. God, he is good. Am I responsible for this? Like attracts like after all. I am indignant.

Everyone is so sure I am the one living in a dream world, but when they all say he'll be back, I think they are in non-reality themselves.

Despite the pain he's caused, I miss his voice and his eyes and his laugh and his smile and the way he says *huh* when he's trying to figure something out. Darn it. This is not what I expected. Ugh. Bring him back please, I pray. I don't think I'd be in more pain if I sliced my finger off with a meat slicer. Honestly. Bring him back and I'll never get in my way again. And to think I gave up Simon too.

*!!***!!***!!*

JUST AS I am mellowing out, Robert calls again. He catches me completely off guard, rips my wounded heart wide open. "What do you want from me?" I plead. "Why do you keep calling? How could you lead me on to think everything was great? How could you lie so easily to me?"

"I'm sorry. I was trying. I really wanted it to work but then I started to think maybe I wasn't really interested in a relationship after all. I don't think it's me."

"Nothing built on lies is." I am angry that the delicate balance of give and take can be abandoned at any moment. Now I need to put my anger on low and let it simmer down. Put a lid on it.

He burned me. As in freezer burn. And nobody likes the taste of that.

Later, in the kitchen, with little provocation, I yell, "Fucking carnivores," catching Georgina's attention. "They're carnivores. The lot of them. They want my blood. I swear. They'd eat me if I was marinated just right."

This is all getting to me. None of it makes sense anymore. Or does it?

"Maybe I should quit while I'm ahead. Cash out. Grow my hair and nails."

"You can't quit all of this over a guy."

"I just can't see myself doing this at fifty. It's a young person's career really."

"I'm young. I'll take it."

"Maybe I can make pretty cookbooks or branch out to party planning—a less physically demanding occupation." It makes sense to blame this on everything else but me, but I could see the irresponsibility in that.

Now that I'd been out playing the game of love, retreating into the safety of my kitchen didn't make sense. My love of food isn't going to nurture me the way a true love could. I hope I'm not eating alone forever.

*!!***!!***!!*

TRY AS I might to forget, I still have a long way to go. Frequent thoughts of him drip onto my day like basted gravy over a turkey. And I am the turkey for letting this happen to me. This is not how I'd planned the menu of our lives together. We went from appetizer to *le justif* without any concern for the main entrée. It was like having a barbecue without the barbecue. Like insulting the whole concept of barbecue by throwing a steak into one of those stove-top pans with grill marks and having the nerve to tell a friend tomorrow that I had barbecue tonight.

Now I am alone. Now I am the pasta without the sauce. The chicken without the skin. The fries without the salt. I torture myself over my conduct. Did I tell too much too soon? Show how smart and savvy I was too soon? Threaten his manhood? Maybe I didn't dumb myself down to him enough.

It means nothing without him, I tell myself moaning, despairingly. What doesn't kill you will make you strong, they say, but I can't hate him for this. I must respect the boundaries he has created for himself, that feel safe around him like the womb he was borne into. I have to stay in love with love somehow and let him go and not be tainted or jaded or frightened.

I am able to cope better with the split-up by pretending he is dead. In this way I can remember what I loved about him and try to forget how he hurt me. I can concentrate on the pain of my loss without a layer of anger choking me.

# Chapter Nine

## Frannie Dover Baby Shower

Cold Buffet Menu for 30
Caramelized Onion, Apple & Walnut Chicken Salad Sandwiches
Curried Egg Salad Sandwiches
Smoked Gouda & Roasted Tomato Sandwiches
Baby Shape Cookies, Baby Carriage Cake
Lemon Ginger Iced Tea, Minted Orange Juice

"Please don't call me Fran. I don't like one syllable names. Especially for myself."

These are the first words I ever hear Frannie Dover say. Then, "My sister-in-law is with child. I'm surprised she's still with my brother as a matter of fact. But here we are. Although I don't much like her, it is my duty to throw her a baby shower. I'm not much into parties. They just seem so silly, and a terrible bore. I don't care what you serve. I should say, however, that I'm not into crudités with dip even if everyone else thinks it's fun and exciting. Everyone thinks the word crudités will make vegetables more than what they plainly are—vegetables. I need food to speak to me. I'm not going to be too interested in what anyone else has to say that day, believe me. Bring me savory sensations instead. Things I'll feel a thrill with. And I'd like the sense of sauce without any of it dripping onto my dress, ruining my attire for the entire afternoon."

"What about food that's fun to eat and fun to look at? Would that help?" I ask, hoping she shares my enthusiasm to be playful, whimsical, even serendipitous in my presentation. "I can cut tea sandwiches into baby shapes. You know, naked babies, little feet, baby carriages, and the like. I think I can even get my hands on some swizzle sticks that look like baby rattles."

"No. That really scares me. Cookies in those shapes are one thing, but sandwiches? No. I think I would lose my appetite. I don't care for the fanfare," Frannie says. "I'm more interested in flavor as I hope you've gathered."

And that was that. Food in celebration of baby making. I'd already thought of my menu—a bit of a standby menu, actually, and easily adaptable for different situations and occasions.

I gave Georgina the week off. She and Philip needed time away together. She was hoping he'd finally pop the question. I was hoping for her sake he did. She promises to be back in time to help me serve the baby shower.

I am in the kitchen, quietly blending my ingredients, little lonely me.

My curried egg salad is simple enough. Just like my life right now. I make sure I don't overboil the eggs and use a combination of cumin and coriander for flavor with a pinch of turmeric for color. My secret is adding goat cheese with the mayonnaise so it isn't too wet. The chicken salad is an accidental recipe from long ago. The caramelized onion really adds a sweet flavor. Coupled with the moist juice from the apple when you chew into it, it's a tasty, tasty dish. I have no doubt Frannie will like it.

Georgina is back in time to decorate the cake and cookies. She has a natural talent we both like to exploit.

I'd bruised the mint leaves much earlier. They'd steeped in the fresh orange juice for more than an hour. I remove the mint and refrigerate the pitcher. It is ready to serve except for the final touch of ice and fresh mint leaves. I do the same with the lemon iced tea, letting ginger infuse itself into the tea for hours.

Frannie comes into the kitchen, looking like she wants to hide, but with more than just that purpose. She notices the mint leaves and brightens instantly. "You have mint. That's great. Do you have sugar cubes with you too?"

"Over there." I point toward her small round breakfast table where I've set up a coffee station.

"This is great." She reaches for a cube with one hand and for the cupboard above her with the other and extracts a martini glass. Vodka appears out of nowhere.

"Okay," I say, "I see where you're going with this. You want something to mash some of those mint leaves with?"

I pass my mortar and pestle to her.

She points the glass at me, her way of asking if I want one too.

"Sure. Why not." Georgina and I had done all the plating we'd need to do for this party. Georgina has set most of the buffet already and is busy with final touches in the living room before we announce the guests can eat. I am cleaning up the kitchen.

"A little break will do you good," Frannie says.

She is skinny, skinny. Not just slender or slim, but downright skinny. She wears a black pencil skirt down to her ankles and a black cotton short-sleeved top she's got belted at the waist. She looks like she is attending a funeral rather than welcoming new life. All the other women are dressed in an array of muted colors and soft pastels, a veritable Monet painting of details. Frannie, however, is a Salvador Dalí—a bold statement against a noncommittal background. Her kitchen is done in black and white ceramic tile and her high heels clack against the hard surface floor as she gathers the ingredients for the martinis. The martini glasses clank on top of the ceramic tile counter.

There are frequent trips to the buffet for Frannie. I know because we bump into each other a few times after we'd shared the martinis in the kitchen. It is refreshing to see she is refilling her plate. She eats silently and with great concentration. She speaks perfunctorily to other guests, but mostly just tries to steal a moment to concentrate on eating. I think such small helpings actually help her focus on the joy of eating. Like having too much food on the plate would drown her; and only a little would make her feel grounded. Her love affair of life is in taste. She guards the little bird helpings on a small side plate, instead of one large meal on a dinner plate like the other women who share the rounded edges of motherhood. There is much excitement with this mother-to-be—her belly too big for her to see her feet. One of the other women notices the lace on one of her yellow Keds is undone and makes a big deal out of tying it for her.

"I think it's time for another break," Frannie suggests.

Once we are privately tucked away in the kitchen again, she says, "So, what's your story? No ring on your finger. No baby to care for either is my guess. Your business is your baby, isn't it? No real room for anyone else, I'd bet. Probably couldn't care less."

"Well, I don't know about that."

"Have you had any relationships lately?"

"I've had a few close calls."

"That's not real enough," she says. She raises her martini glass to mine and we toast. "You're not ready. I can see you're not there yet."

My conversation with Frannie does not interfere with a conversation I'm having with myself at the same time. I'm envisioning singular visions of my future. I am at the food convention alone. I am eating a restaurant dinner *au solitaire.* I'm drinking a whole shaker of martinis alone.

"I want him."

"Who?"

"My boyfriend. Ex."

"Where is he?"

"He's dead."

"Oh, my, how did he die?"

"Well, he's not really dead. I'm just pretending he's dead to make myself feel better."

"Is it working?"

"I don't know."

"Yeah, but what does he want? He probably doesn't have the first clue. Most men pull us in and push us away simultaneously. I'm done with them. I've been beaten. I've been threatened. I don't know why. It goes bad and then they want to kill me. I must rub them the wrong way. After the last one, the last two, I'm done. I'm better off on my own. It's safer. What happened with your guy? He didn't try to kill you, too, did he?"

"No. At least not literally."

I don't want to think about his negative traits, even if he did string me along and lie to me. No one's perfect after all.

I'd never let my guard down with a client before. Never taken more than one drink on a job. Frannie has a talent with those minted martinis though. By the end of the afternoon, all those baby-celebrating women have cooed and oohed enough for us both. We are firmly planted in the kitchen. Georgina is the front man and runs the party without us.

The oohs and aahs and high-pitched laughs are a world away from the kitchen. All the pinks and yellows and baby blues finally dismantle from the living room and return to their soft cotton lives.

I am very pleased with our efforts and am directing Georgina to wrap the leftovers when Frannie comes in and screams. Not an outright scream that startles me, but a loud gasp, really. Georgina cuts me a glance that says, *Frannie's your new best friend. Handle it.*

Before I can say anything, Frannie says, "No leftovers. None. What are you trying to do? Fatten me up? Tonight was my night. Tomorrow is another day and I need an empty fridge. Fruit. Vegetables. Okay. But no cheese, no sauces, no flavor embellishments. You can't tempt me that way. Just throw it all out or take it home with you. Give it away on the street corner for all I care. How can anything so fattening be called salad anyway?" she asks.

"So you'd like me to dispose of everything?"

"You betcha."

By the time Georgina and I are finished, I am shocked to find I am too drunk to drive.

"Georgina," I whisper to her, a little off balance, swaying even, catching my balance on the tile counter, "I think you need to drive us back to the kitchen."

"What are you doing? I've never seen you like this. I think you've done enough today. Yeah, I'll drive the Lip-Mobile. I'll take you home. You're sure not going to be any good to me tomorrow."

"Oh, stop busting my chops and get me out of here.

"I want a simple, clearly understood liaison," I say. "I'm not going to wait until after I've slept with him to ask what he wants out of a relationship. I don't want to hear someone tell me they're not looking for anything serious, or that they don't want to marry, or that they really enjoy their single life and just want someone to play with occasionally. Fuck that. Let them find a twenty-two-year-old with all the time in the world on their hands who doesn't understand how quickly time passes. Fuck the man who can't decide. Then leave him. Quickly. And don't look back. And don't, definitely don't, return his phone call if he calls again. Fuck him for not knowing what he wants."

"God, Gwen, what's happened to you?"

"I want to break bread with someone for the rest of my life. Why is that so hard to manage? Why am I left alone all the time?" I was whining now, talking to the window.

"You're too capable. Too independent. Probably too frightened and insecure if you ask me."

"I didn't ask. I was speaking to the window. I've been able to create happy clients who are loyal, why not a happy counterpart?" I moan out loud.

Georgina pulls up to the curb in front of my house and leaves me to fend for myself. "I'm not going to help you to your door. I have a lot to do in the kitchen."

"What a huge slap on the universal face of love. If the sex were bad it'd be easy to forget him," I say to myself on the walk to my door.

Safely, but not soundly, tucked into my home, I concede that Frannie might be right. If I were ready it would be here already. Obviously my relationship to relationships would have to change.

# Chapter Ten

## Mrs. Maple's Afternoon Tea

Cold Buffet Menu for 12
Assorted Tea Sandwiches:
Albacore Tuna & Raisin, Egg & Tarragon,
Zucchini Bread & Mesquite Turkey
Banana Bread, Shortbread Cookies, Lemon Bars
Tea & Coffee Service

I am nursing a headache the next morning, a little queasy admittedly. I take a cab over to the kitchen to pick up my car and then drive to Frannie's to pick up final payment for the party, forgotten yesterday. She spots me from her living room window and motions for me to come in. She has a mug of coffee in her hand and lifts it toward me—universal language for *do you want one?* I walk up the front path and enter her home. There's no sign of yesterday's party. Not even the tiniest piece of ribbon is left to tell the day-after tale. If I'd not been there myself, I would not have believed it. She knows I can't handle much noise right now. A cup is poured for me by the time I get into the kitchen.

"You look a little rough around the edges," she says, and pushes the sugar and creamer my way.

"I'm too busy to be hungover right now. Those were damn good drinks though."

"Decent party considering."

"Thanks."

"I really regret letting you throw all that food out. By midnight I was craving your chicken salad in a big bad way."

"Most do once they've tried it. Thanks for the coffee. Just the right amount of strong and fresh."

*!!***!!***!!*

I'm struck by sunlight that hits my forehead like a hammer as I drive over to Lip Service; the pain of it lingers along my temples for hours. To make matters worse, I'm on the phone back and forth all day with indecisive Mrs. Maple when I get there. My head is spinning. This is supposed to be an easy month, but at this rate, with two of Mrs. Maple's functions back-to-back, I'd be cooked in no time. Oh. And her short attention span? Ouch. I have two files going at once. My pencil is sharpened. We have to get this done.

Mrs. Maple's on the board of a nonprofit called the Foundation for Children's Artistic Endeavors. It grants monies to after-school programs in community centers around Los Angeles. Art and music education are big since these activities are less and less present in schools. I have not one, but two events with her this month. We jump between the plans for the tea party at her house in Bel-Air and the fundraiser at a gallery downtown.

We fine-tune plans for the yearly fundraiser. We order and reorder linens. I am determined to pin her down on color by sundown. My reluctance to change the order again and again hasn't stopped her from clocking more time against my profits.

Mrs. Maple hosts the biyearly board meeting at her house on Mapleton Drive. She loves my tea party setup. Her merry bunch of teetotalers and fellow board members never miss it. They always want the same menu. Light sandwiches and tea breads. The breads and desserts are delish, but it is the presentation that takes it all to a new level. English bone china in pretty mismatched patterns, handcrafted mini tea cozies to wrap small individual teapots, and globally sourced organic tea blends in little treasure chest boxes. The shortbread is a very traditional recipe that the gang at Marks & Spencer's would no doubt approve of. They make a delightful complement to the tea service.

*!!***!!***!!*

I AM withdrawn and reticent, still wincing from Frannie's insights. Putting myself into a vacuum, I go to work. I cook. I go home. Georgina notices but is tight-lipped and doesn't want to cross the boundary of my pain. Mine becomes a simple life. An agonized, self-incriminating life of anxious debate. What am I trying to prove anyway? It might be better to not want so much. Singledom. Ugh. I wasn't exactly desperate, but I was insecure. I'd lost my footing.

Genevieve would be back. She'd want Hermie, and Hermie wasn't. Not anymore. It was possible she wasn't going to be my friend anymore either.

I take solace in preparing the baked goods for Mrs. Maple's afternoon tea. Baking is an exact science and I appreciate the narrow confines of its parameters. In baking you can't add something without taking something away.

"I'm going to bake both the zucchini bread and banana bread in mini Bundt pans to give them some height in their presentation, Georgina. Will you handle the shortbread?"

"Of course." She uses the voice of someone offering condolences, but she gets right to work. She pulls flour, butter, preps the mixer. "Will you talk about it?" She presses, "I know you're still not over Robert. It's going to take time. At least you know yourself better, and you know what you want now."

"Do you know how lame that sounds? Not to mention I doubt it's true." I say to Georgina later, "It was such a waste of time."

She coddles me. "I've never thought of a relationship as a waste. You'll always be able to take something with you. Don't ever think it's a waste of time," she replies.

"How are things with Philip?"

"Ho hum so-so."

She proceeds to complain about him in an "it isn't what it's cracked up to be" way to make me feel better.

I want to complain that she isn't appreciating what she has. Philip is coming home to her every night, thinking of what she might need on his way back from the office, considering her when he makes plans. Taking so much for granted, she complains instead about how he keeps the light on at night so he can read a few pages, a tiff she picks with him often, she confesses with remorse, like she has every right to demand a dark room for sleepy time. No, no, it is he who is the sinning culprit as far as she can see.

"You need to get out there again," is Georgina's advice.

I'd get back out there when the time was right. No need to push up against it all.

*!!***!!***!!*

Mrs. Maple's house is deep in exclusive Bel-Air, has stone sides and crisscross-patterned windows. It is exquisite, complete with a service entrance, and while I know I am providing a service today, I resent being sent around to the side entrance like I'm not good enough to come through the front door. There is just too much pomp and circumstance here for my taste today. Her guests include a small collection of aged women, all of whom had used their marriages and subsequent divorces to further themselves financially.

Oh, they'd paid the price, I'd heard them all say in so many words. They'd birthed children they had no relationship with today. They'd gone into marriages thinking all was good, their intentions in the right place because a voice in the back of their heads said they couldn't figure out a way to do it without a man, they hadn't thought of a way to make a living like their husbands could. I hadn't actually heard them utter this truth, but I could read it in their faces like I could read my planned menu for the day.

Their lives have been reduced to simple, but pampered pleasures and the frequent social gatherings that have food at their center. They are a comfort food loving bunch. They wear warm soft knits and heavy makeup and long-chained jewelry that hangs over their sweater sets. It is hard to tell them apart. Mrs. Maple always has the same roundup of women colleagues. They bore me senseless.

"I hope there's banana bread today," Phyllis says each and every time we cater this small event, her hair coiffed in stiff wavy curls. Every time, she uses a napkin and wraps herself a piece for her morning coffee the next day, sneaking it into her pocket, thinking we don't notice. Cassandra is more into the lemon squares, turning her nose up at the banana bread to the delight of Phyllis. More for her pocket, I can see her thinking. More for me, me, me.

These are all women who walked away from their marriages with little financial worry, pushing upon their ex-husbands a new sense of lack.

"Are these women scary, or is it me?" I whisper to Georgina.

"Oh, they're harmless."

"I'll bet their kids wouldn't agree."

"Like you know."

"I think they're trying to make amends for their neglect."

"Keep that up you may be in hot water. You should check the tea kettle."

*!!***!!***!!*

I'M IN hot water all right. Genevieve and Dan have barely docked at Marina del Rey when they are on my doorstep, rat-a-tat-tatting their own version of a bird call on my window. Hermie was a goner. I might be a goner if I opened the door, but I was pulling it open anyway. And here they are, all smiles and happiness. Sunshine and possibility. Genevieve has a direct view of the cage that emits no sound. There isn't much that I can say so I let the heaviness fall into the room and sink around us.

"What happened?" she asks, but she knows. Her eyes cloud over.

Even Dan gets teary while reaching for the cage.

"I can't say for sure. He was fine. I loved having him. I wish he was still here."

*!!***!!***!!*

I DEFINITELY need some time to heal. I realize if I'd been interested in a mere boyfriend, I'd have someone already. The rules of engagement had changed, now that I had actually set my intention, it would be necessary to weed my way through all sorts of men again. I'd gone from one extremely measured extreme to another—from finding all men sufficient to knowing only one could do it for me. No wonder it feels so futile. I am in a pool with men who have searched for only one woman. As tempted as I might be normally, these are men who had already built an immunity to the likes of me. There'd be no romancing the stone, no testing the waters, no walking the thin line. No flirting with disaster. There'd be no nookie for me. I just didn't know how anyone managed to get married at all. These are the thoughts that plague my awareness before I succumb to sleep.

I wake throughout the night. The moon has moved across the sky and upon each waking, I chart its journey from its brightest phase to its darkest, most hidden state, asleep without sleeping. Just like me.

*!!***!!***!!*

I AGREE to meet with Mrs. Maple even though everything could be done over the phone. Enough of the fundraiser is organized already, but she likes to hold an audience with people and actually have a meeting. I know deep down I am her cure for loneliness today. When I arrive at her stately home on Mapleton Drive—this time through the front door she's left open for me—I find her in the study with the *Los Angeles Times* Sunday newspaper and a pair of scissors.

"I'm the victim of a coupon war," she says.

"Let me tell you something about coupons, Mrs. Maple. All the time you spend clipping them in order to save a few cents isn't worth it. How much is your time worth after all? That's all I'm going to say about it."

"You could be right, dear Gwen. But I do love to think I'm bargain shopping. Which brings me to the fundraiser. I don't want to spend a lot of money on the food. My intention is to make money, not lose it."

"Goodness no. It's the art that will fill them. They'll virtually be surrounded by it, won't they?"

"Yes. We're hanging the children's art around the walls and auctioning it off at eight P.M."

"It's probably best to do tray-passed hors d'oeuvres."

"Passed sparingly while you're at it, please. And we need to think of something for the youngsters."

"Maybe pigs in a blanket or mini corn dogs."

"That sounds good—and filling. Whichever is cheaper."

"I'd like to do crab cakes, crumb-encrusted brie, brandied mushroom caps, and some caramelized onion phyllo cups."

"Good heavens. Those sound sophisticated and expensive. Is there any way to keep the cost down?"

"I can make it work."

"If only there were coupons for half-off wine and beer in the newspaper. I know I can't get away without the beer and wine bar."

"Not if you want happy hands writing checks."

"We must preserve the arts."

"I have a varied supply of discount wines on hand we can use. We can stretch your dollar by running the bar for only an hour and waiting to run the bulk of the food afterward. It'll be cheaper for you if guests arrive late."

Once Mrs. Maple approves my menu ideas, she says, "I'd like all the food to be gone by the time the auction begins so it doesn't interfere with the guests buying great art."

"I don't think that will be a problem."

I sell Mrs. Maple on hors d'oeuvres that are already in my freezer that I made weeks ago for just this kind of event. They represent pure profit for me.

I still call Nadine to round things out. "Nadine, have you got anything new on the horizon?"

"Are you thinking appetizers or main dish? Local or imported?"

"I was thinking budget friendly desserts. Local. We're doing a bar service and appetizers. I already have some of your breaded mushroom caps, mini encrusted brie, and crab cakes in the freezer. I'm setting up a portable deep fryer."

"You really take mobile to a new level. I've got these sheet pies you might like."

"Is that like a sheet cake, but a pie instead?"

"Pretty much. They just came in. No complaints yet."

"Okay."

"They come in four flavors so if you've got a big crowd you can offer a nice variety."

*!!***!!***!!*

WHAT A perfect pair they are. He likes the insides of the pie. She likes the crust. Together they're the whole damn pie. Apple, cherry, and strawberry rhubarb. If I have to witness the beginning of someone else's happily ever after, I am going to toss my lunch all over the floor. Why them and not me? Why I let Georgina talk me into lunch at Marie Callender's, I'll never know. Not only did I have to listen to her love story, I am enviously watching one unfold in front of my very own eyes. This lunch is supposed to pull me out of my funk not encase me in it.

What you read into it is also part of the story and in my story, they live happily ever after. Mr. and Mrs. Piecrust.

The only thing interesting about this lunch is the lone tall dark and handsome sitting at the counter. *He's the type of guy I'd sleep with right away and then drop like a hot potato*, I think to myself. And just like that I am ready to start again.

# Chapter Eleven

## Foundation for Children's Artist Endeavors Fundraiser

Tray-Passed Hors d'Oeuvres Menu for 500
Crab Cakes, Mushroom Caps, Crumb-Encrusted Brie
Apple, Cherry, Strawberry Rhubarb Mini Pie Squares

Now that I've been out in the world playing the game of love, I know I can't go back and retreat into the safety of my kitchen. My sequestered heart would need to be freed. My love of food isn't going to nurture me in the way that a true love can. I am ready to go out and have fun and sleep with strangers like I used to. I need the loving touch of a skillful lover. I am ready to try again.

With so little to do before Mrs. Maple's event, I decide to explore new options at Great Expectations. Off I go to the selection chamber. I hit the binders again and think James might be fun for a while. Or Edward. Or both. I am just going to go out with all of them. In a couple of months, I'll see them for who they really are and will be able to make a decision based on facts, not on the hormonal trappings of lust.

I need a cure for my own loneliness. I want someone to put his face between my legs to drink his fill of me. I need to put something in there. Not a penis to be found anywhere and I am without my vibrator. My body is hungry for something to fill it. I would suck my own breast if I could and quench my own desires.

I want to lie on my belly and spread my legs for him, my unseen lover, and feel his hands on my buttocks. Stir against the bed, my nipples aroused by his touch. I can hear his panting breath as I feel him climb deeper and deeper into me—with a rushed surrender I grit my teeth against. I am going to melt. I will burst if he doesn't take me. My hand crosses my mouth to silence my cry. I will close my eyes so I don't know who he is and wrap my legs around him.

*!!***!!***!!*

DOUBTING THOMAS has no doubt I'm the one for him. I dub him Doubting Thomas when several of my own doubts about him surface. I waited and waited to have sex with him because I'd seen a lot of red flags. I figure with my doubts, we'd be better off friends.

He always takes the smallest of everything. The smallest cookie. The smallest muffin. Even the smallest mug for his coffee in the morning. It's like he's afraid of the biggest. One morning I pour his coffee from the small mug down the drain, reach for the largest mug available and fill it with fresh coffee, just to see how he reacts. "There," I say, "you need a larger cup. Live life large." *Please*.

He is puzzled by my behavior. I see the way he looks into the tall mug like it's a deep ocean he won't plunge into, afraid of his own emotional depths. I'm trying to give him the benefit of the doubt for the sake of being in a relationship, but my doubts won't be ignored.

I'm stalking him in my own way too. Not directly, but indirectly, I am secretly on his trail. A snoop as it were. Opening cupboards and drawers during my visits to his apartment while he's in the bathroom. Peeking, touching, lifting. *Shame on me*, I think over and over again, as I continue my search for something that gives me all the information I need, to stop this nonsense and go home. How could I possibly reduce myself to this?

He has his meals all mixed up as well. He eats cereal for dinner and dinner foods for breakfast. It disturbs me.

When we do get around to sex, he doesn't last longer than it takes to boil a soft-boiled egg. Less than three minutes and my breakfast? I prefer my eggs hard-boiled, smeared in butter and salt.

"I don't understand why it didn't work between the two of you," Genevieve asks weeks later when I run into her at Barnes & Noble. Dan is with her. They'd been in the travel magazine section when she sees me breezing through to the cookbook section. She pulls me aside to get the details.

"Let's put it this way, he likes to spoon, and I like to fork. Let's leave it at that," I say.

*!!***!!***!!*

MY THOUGHTS are on Edward all day. He's the shining star in this recent array of possibilities. I haven't even met him yet and I'm already fantasizing about how perfect we are for each other. I decide it would be best if he came by and ate dinner with me. On Friday. Say around seven o'clock. I can pull some of the stuffed chicken from the freezer and put together a very nice salad with hearts of palm and sun-dried tomatoes. I debate on whether the starch portion of the meal should be a potato dish or rice. My basil rice would be a nice complement to the meal.

He would spend the night but not before we'd had a talk about us. And he would only spend the night if I were happy with what he had to say for himself. I guess it would have been nice to let him know that he was even invited before I'd made so many presumptions. But they seemed so doable and I couldn't imagine him not going along with them.

He says he can't make it. He's not available. Imagine my dismay. His words sting as much as they might if he'd accepted the invitation and then called an hour ahead of time to say he couldn't come. In my mind that's exactly what he'd done. Poor guy. He just can't win. It isn't a simple rejection to my dinner invitation. It's a total rejection of everything I might be to him. He is accused and prosecuted before he even knows he's a suspect. I really need to examine my approach. Is it another self-sabotaging tendency of mine? Purposely thwarting my own happiness by contributing to definite disappointment? Could very well be. We reschedule.

*!!***!!***!!*

"Let me tell you what I don't like. Bratwurst." I say this to Edward on the way over to the restaurant. Bratwurst is the special of the night. Of course. He eats three square meals a day. Doesn't even wait to get hungry. I learn this while we wait for our table—and he loves bratwurst.

We talk and talk, so at ease with each other. An obvious connection. Dinner comes and goes, our plates are cleared, the table is crummy.

"Dessert anyone?" our waitress asks as she presents the entire dessert tray, temptingly.

"Not for me," he says. He doesn't let her offer me anything. The waitress retreats.

Red flag.

"Sugar's going to kill us all," he says and leans in closer. "I've removed it from my diet altogether. Not a trace of it."

*So now I have to live without it?* Red flag.

"Was it hard to give up?"

"It took months. I read a lot of labels. It's one thing to give up blatantly obvious sources of sugar like candy and pastry—it's all the invisible sugar I had to work hard to eliminate. Salad dressing, even a seemingly healthy granola bar. Sugar's everywhere. It's the invisible demon. Do you realize 'no sugar added' doesn't really mean that at all? A company can have trace elements in a product and still label it 'no sugar added.' I think it's a conspiracy to deaden our senses. Food manufacturing companies, the FDA, the Medical Association—they're all in on it. I'm sure of it. I see signs of it all the time."

Red flag.

*!!***!!***!!*

TRUTH BE told, deep down, I expect to be disappointed. What a terrible thing to know that. I expect him to disappoint me, maybe even annoy me. I expect him to not be anything like his profile promises. Not the manly man I'd hoped for. Not as tall as he'd written he was, and certainly not as nice. I expect him to tell me he's looking for a long-term commitment and then change his mind three months into the relationship, long after I've committed every fragmented piece of my heart to him.

I expect to still be alone on Friday and Saturday nights even though he is supposed to be my boyfriend and we are supposed to have plans on those nights like most couples. I expect to wake up alone in the morning because he suddenly can't sleep by my side. I am too hot. I hog the covers. I roll over too often and it is disturbing his peaceful slumber. I expect him to get up in the middle of the night and dress and smack an obligatory kiss on my cheek when I ask him groggily, *"Where are you going?"* I expect to not be surprised when he answers, *"I'm going home to my own bed where I can get a good night's sleep."*

I expect to try not to feel used after we'd made love only hours before and that couldn't even keep him in my bed. I expect all this and more and I hadn't even met him. All this and I didn't even seem bitter on the outside. I did not yet resemble a loaf of bread—crusty on the outside, soft on the inside. No, I still look like I give a shit, and all of this is of great interest to me. I still look like a sucker lining up for more. I still look like there is hope for me.

*!!***!!***!!*

THE GALLERY for the Foundation for Children's Artistic Endeavors fundraiser is a large and industrial loft downtown—a lot of steel grey and metal—not a patch of grass to be found for miles. There is only one tree there, right out front, dug into the ground with cement poured all around it. Georgina and I are going to do a walk-through of the space to make sure we have ordered the right tables for the space constraints. A vagrant is peeing on the tree when we arrive.

"Let's call Giuseppe to protect us the night of the event," I say.

*!!***!!***!!*

I BEG off work early so I can meet James for coffee.

"I'm so nervous on first dates," he says. "I drank too much coffee today. I usually only have one cup in the morning when I read the paper, but today—well, I was so, so nervous I don't know what happened. Before I knew it, I'd ordered another cup with breakfast and stopped for one on the way home. I guess I was tired and—well—wanted to have a little pick-me-up. I didn't want you to think I was asleep at the wheel boring. Oh, and now you probably think I'm a java junkie. Really, I'm just nervous. I haven't dated in a long time. I'm not even sure how to do it. Oh, maybe we should talk about you. I really liked your profile. I thought we had so much in common when I read it. Thanks for meeting me—for coming here today. I couldn't even imagine what a good first date would be. You really are beautiful. I like your short hair. I've never really liked long hair. I know some men find it sexy and erotic but I think it just gets in the way. Maybe it's because I like necks. I'm a neck man. Not that I don't like breasts or legs, it's just that—well—I don't know. I just like seeing and touching necks. Anyway, now that that's out of the way, do you want to have sex?"

"Do you mind if I finish my coffee?"

*!!***!!***!!*

GIUSEPPE CINOLIO, my bodyguard for hire, comes to protect us while we unload our goods into the art gallery. He's big in every direction and does a great job holding open doors and looking serious. It's already dark on the streets of LA and we aren't taking any chances.

Giuseppe—aka Gigi Goon—(but don't call him that to his face unless he's given you permission) is already a big help with a couple of dubious-looking characters on the corner. They are probably just hungry, but I have enough mouths to feed tonight. I don't have to worry about threats to my life or Georgina's life with Gigi around. He applied for one of my waitstaff positions several months ago, but his tough guy looks really work for this venue. He makes a good wage as a waiter, but as a protector he gets a bump for the night and still shares in the tip pool.

We set up our kitchen quickly—the rental company arrives at the same moment we do and unloads the portable canvas walls into the far corner and within minutes the tables are up—another way Gigi comes in handy. We push the warming ovens into place.

Mrs. Maple is dressed in a hand-painted-canvas pantsuit that makes her look like an Henri Matisse piece on the move.

The artwork hangs by fishing line suspended in midair with black velvet backing it and museum light illuminating it. Her coveted would-be musicians are setting up on an elevated platform in the center of the room, already surrounded by the same black velvet cloth. Some of the artwork is clearly elementary with bright primary colors and an innocence that is certainly childlike, and then some of it seems so advanced it is hard to believe a child had painted it at all.

"Maybe it's their inner adult running amuck," Georgina says.

"That would explain everything," I reply and set about the task of food preparation.

I am nearly convinced the evening would prove successful, but who am I to judge. It's Mrs. Maple and her canvas-lined pockets that will know for sure.

It isn't going to be a particularly busy night for us. The hors d'oeuvres selection is scarce and considering how many guests are to be served, the food won't go far. The real finesse in an event like this is in timing. The servers enter the crowd only once it has nearly swelled to its expected capacity and when they do serve, the platters are not filled, they are airily displayed, forcing them to return time and time again to refill their platters. It gives the illusion of plenty, but really most would starve here tonight. If the guests had any sense, they'd have eaten at the Brewery or one of the other downtown eateries before arriving.

The crowd is swelling, children and their eager parents are here to see their children's work. The musicians begin to play classical music and as the night advances, their choices turn to pop and light rock and finally to rhythm and blues. They are good enough to make me want to dance and that is a rare deal these days.

I can see from my perch at the corner of the kitchen that some of the youngsters are following the servers and demanding more brie and mushroom caps like uncultured pearls in a deep sea. Georgina notices, too, and before I can do anything about it, she zeroes in, saying, "Now take one for each hand and scat. We've more than your mouths to fill tonight."

We are nearing the end of our passes; cleanup will begin shortly. Cleanup is easy when the food's all gone—it's just packing up platters and wrapping up garbage at that point. And Gigi Goon is eager to help with the dirty work. The rental company will pick up their stuff as soon as the event ends. I am pretty much done for the night. I give Mrs. Maple a high sign when we'd done our last pass.

Mrs. Maple makes her introductions and mentions her board members and their invaluable help for preparing for this yearly event and gets right down to the business of auctioning off the artwork. The room falls to a hushed silence as bidding commences at $500 for the first piece.

"Let's not forget what a worthy cause this is," she says. "Do I hear $600? Yes, thank you. Seven hundred? One thousand dollars? Excellent." And on it goes until Mrs. Maple's voice turns scratchy and nearly all the art is gone. Then the Rembrandt knock-off portraitist's work comes up.

I notice the first portrait looks an awful lot like the man standing next to me.

"Hey, is that you?" I ask him before I can stop myself.

"Yes, my nephew's the painter. He talked me into it one Sunday morning when I thought we'd be playing soccer together. He was inspired by my choice of shirt that day and I was cornered before I knew it. It was the pressure from my sister that really did me in though."

"It's a shocking resemblance. Not shocking as in bad though—shocking as in striking. He's really good, isn't he?"

"The crowd seems to think so—the bidding's already over $1,000. I may blush if it gets much higher. My name's Jack."

"My name's Gwen. I'm the caterer. You probably missed my food. It practically evaporated off the platters it was gone so fast."

"Yeah, we ate at the Brewery."

"Smart move."

"I think I'm going to make a dash for it before anyone else recognizes me. I'm not used to the limelight. Is there a rear entrance?"

I point toward Gigi and give him the sign to let Jack through.

"Do you have a card? Can I call you sometime?"

"Yeah, sure you can."

"You're single then?"

"Like you don't even know."

Despite myself I like him. Despite every bad thing that has happened to me I am hopeful this just might work—at least the first date or the second date. I can't see beyond that right now.

I'd saved a small sampling of the menu for my staff and when Gigi comes to check in, he catches sight of what is left of the brie.

"Oh, look at that brie. Can I put it on my plate?"

"That is your plate," I reply, handing it to him and kissing him on the cheek. "Thanks for saving my life tonight," I say.

"I didn't save your life. Nothing happened."

"See what I mean?" I say. "You saved my life. Nothing happened."

# Chapter Twelve

## Prefab Fabulous Holiday Menu for Everyone

Chèvre, Garlic, Cranberry, Herb & Pine Nut Infused Whole Chickens
With Breadless Stuffing
Honey Ham with Candied Pineapple & Blood Orange Sauce
Polenta with Sautéed Arugula, Roasted Tomatoes with
Chipotle Tomato Sauce
Garlic Green Beans
Salad of Mixed Greens with Avocado, Sun-dried Tomatoes,
Chèvre & Toasted Pine Nuts
tossed in Tarragon Vinaigrette
Holiday Cookie Platter

By the time I hear from Jack, I'd already given up on casual dating. Even my desires for a life of wedded bliss are on the back burner. I come to terms with the idea I may just be a career woman after all. I am in my office late on Wednesday night when he calls. I'm revamping my party menus and planning a makeover for my kitchen and office. It isn't until Jack mentions art that I even knew who he is. We talk for several minutes.

"How does it feel to have fetched the highest price at the show?"

"I credit the artist over the subject on that piece of art. In fact, he's so good he's got a booth at the Venice Art Walk with some of his classmates. Would you like to come? That's why I'm calling. It's not because I'm hungry or have a party to throw."

We determined neither of us is afraid of early mornings and decide to meet for breakfast at Ivy at the Shore. From there we'd head over to the boardwalk before the inevitable crowds move in.

When I look at Jack, I see an attractive, middle-aged man who is sure of himself, but not overbearingly so. I like his quiet confidence.

"You haven't mentioned what you do for a living," I say once our breakfast is on the table.

"I'm an architect. My dad taught me a lot when I was growing up. It seemed natural to follow in his footsteps."

He removes his sports jacket and places the cloth napkin on his lap. He uses his fork to cut through his chilaquiles after dousing them with salsa.

He has a house over near the Pacific Design Center in West Hollywood and an impressive list of clients. He has a gentle nature and although I find him attractive, I'm not thinking about a relationship, so I am reluctant to acknowledge any temptation I may have noticed, let alone act on it. We are sharing breakfast, taking a walk, and browsing for art. I'm happy enough with the idea of making a new friend.

The stores aren't open yet so there aren't many cars around. Our walk into Venice is undisturbed except for the occasional cyclist zooming by.

The mixed media of art is impressive. I'd seen this show a couple times in the past, but it seems more colorful as Jack's sidekick. His design background gives him an instant appreciation of color and line displayed in the art, and I find myself looking at it all through his eyes. I stop in my tracks when I see the kitchen art at the end of the second aisle of booths. Twenty-by-twenty-inch canvases oozing with the rich palette of exotic fruits make my mouth water and I instantly wonder why I haven't put more fruit salads on the menu. The pieces make me rethink my kitchen makeover. I want pomegranate-colored walls and a papaya-colored ceiling.

Jack has the impressive ability to read my mind without my ever opening my mouth.

"I think you should buy all of them."

"I was just thinking I was certain my world wouldn't be complete without them on my walls."

"You should decorate a whole room around them. The dining room or maybe even your kitchen. I specialize in kitchens."

"Do you?"

"No, but, given enough time, I could specialize in you and learn everything I need to know about kitchens."

In my previous life I let things progress rapidly, especially with a major hint like that, but now I am moving in a slow motion I didn't know possible.

He slaps a deposit on the artwork so we can walk the rest of the show together unencumbered. Eventually we make our way back to his truck and then drive back to pick up the canvases; the artist is tickled she's able to keep them in a series.

*!!***!!***!!*

DAYS LATER Jack invites himself to my kitchen so he can see what I am up to. Little did I know he wants to impose his design style on my workspace. He has some good ideas, ones I never considered.

"Why don't you take a wall down here, and put up a wall there, and add a tasting room for clients. You do that, don't you? Clients come in to try things before they commit to letting you do their party, don't they?"

"I like the sound of a tasting room. Very clever. But taking down walls sounds loud and messy. And dirty."

"You could hire an after-hours crew and seal off the kitchen to make it work during business hours."

I can understand how his business is so successful. He seems to assess things quickly and his mind works at lightning speed. He wants to give, to share, and before long, he has seeped into every corner of my life.

"Are you looking for a girlfriend?" I ask one day, after he has drawn preliminary plans for a kitchen makeover even Martha might drool over.

I feel completely justified in asking. I can't push up against this and be disappointed again. I want to get to know him before the physical sets in. I want to know how safe I am in his arms.

"I wasn't looking for a girlfriend until you came along."

Despite myself I like him and want to know more. Despite every bad thing that has happened to me I am hopeful this just might work. I soak him in like saliva into cotton candy, and meltingly memorize all I like about him.

He must have known not to push himself on me in an intimate way. He is appealing to my professional side and slowly winning my heart. Eventually I kiss him because I appreciate him so much. It is a dark and warm place—his mouth—and I am glad to go there.

We start to build our lives around each other. I let him talk me into letting him redesign my kitchen and oversee the renovations in the lull after Christmas.

We split our time pretty evenly between my house and his. Parking is never easy in West Hollywood, but he parks his car on the street and lets me have his short driveway on the nights I spend with him. He meets me at the door with the most luscious kisses that lead into an exotic reprieve I have no choice but to surrender to. He makes me feel naked even with clothes on, but those first few months they are mostly off, living a lonely life on the floor beneath us.

I grow accustomed to his spacious, airy, Zen-den living space and our breakfasts at Urth Caffé. He grows accustomed to finding a work area in my study by pushing my cookbooks out of the way and taking his late-night business calls there with his feet resting on the rolling ottoman.

I grow to rely on him in ways I wouldn't have expected from myself. I have eyes for only him. We live with plans extended far out into the future. He quenches my every desire. I can't help but dream of marrying him during these slumbering moments, but I can't entertain it during my waking hours. I don't want to jinx it.

"Let's have some of our friends over for Christmas."

"I'm in if you're in. We can entertain here."

*!!***!!***!!*

My schedule fills in quickly for the holiday season. In years past I booked parties without concern for how they ate up my own holiday plans, but this year is different. I decide to offer one menu only, and easily sell the same menu to a number of different clients. It cuts down on time at my desk crunching numbers and swapping entrée ideas back and forth and makes ordering and prepping a breeze. My plan is to package everything already prepared in easy-to-heat disposables and deliver them to clients on Christmas Eve morning. Clients will just reheat as per my instructions on the top of the package. My wheat-free stuffing becomes an instant hit for the weight-conscious-holiday-dreading crowd as a sumptuous and satisfying accompaniment to the stuffed chickens I planned to make. And while the ham sounds plain, it is melt-in-your-mouth sweetness.

Among the lineup is Frannie Dover. She shrieks when I describe the stuffing.

"Finally, someone is on my side. How do you think the meal will taste with martinis?"

"Make pomegranate or cranberry martinis. It'll be fabulous."

Wynn Zimmerman doesn't want his wife to cook so he is an easy sell, but I have to go over how everything will be prepared and dissect the stuffing for the chicken while his wife takes notes. She talks me into dropping everything off in earthenware dishes she swears she'll return. She won't be admitting to her guests that she hasn't cooked.

Sophia and Clarence Richmond are huge fans of prefab fabulous prepared entrées. I can hear Clarence in the background when I am going over the menu with Sophia.

"Is that Gwen, Sophia? Sophia, tell her I still dream about the meal she did for my birthday party. Have her bring two of everything. We'll feast for days."

"Did you get that, Gwen?" Sophia asks with a laugh in her voice.

I adore them.

"I'll send as much as you want. Tell Clarence he'll have to go easy on the cookies and share them with you."

Georgina and I sail through the prep with the cooking channel blaring show after show in the true spirit of holiday cooking. Sara Moulton, Sandra Lee, The Barefoot Contessa, and even Paula Deen are all making our mouths water and our spirits soar.

Georgina is well-versed with polenta and makes it from scratch. She rolls it into rounds and then cuts it to make spheres of golden cakes, fries them crisp on the outside but leaves them tender on the inside. I can eat them like oversized corn chips all day long. I busy myself with the stuffing mixture for the chicken—huge amounts of garlic and chèvre are already in a bowl as I pick through a small pile of fresh sage, tarragon, and chives. Reducing the dried cranberries to small pieces is the hardest task of the day. Even though they are soft on the inside, their skins are hard to break down. I have to start by grinding them in my food processor and then hand chopping them to get them to the desired size.

"Well fa-la-la-la finally," I mutter when I am done.

"I'm going to start on the cookie dough. I'll do the shortbread first so it can chill before I send it through the press and onto the cookie sheets," Georgina announces.

"What did you get Philip for Christmas?"

"He's a bit on the practical side. He gave me a list to work from—not very romantic at all. It was mostly gadgetry. One-stop shopping at Radio Shack and Circuit City. What did you get Jack?"

"Among other things, I bought him a nice collection of architectural books showcasing some of the best architects in the world and wrapped them in stately paper. I think he'll appreciate them."

"So you're steeping him in romanticism, too, huh? What do you think he's getting you?"

"Haven't got a clue. I'm happy with my new kitchen."

"How do you want to deliver all these meals?"

"Carlos offered to do it for tips."

"That's unusually generous of him."

"Well, he knows our clients will be generous this time of year."

*!!***!!***!!*

I DECIDE to give Jack the books as my Christmas Eve present to him. They are waiting on the nightstand as I sink into bed. He catches me off guard with the ring. He put it in a large box and presents it once I am in bed. We haven't talked about an engagement at all, although we are practically living together. Once I see the ring, my confidence wavers. The books are not nearly as impressive.

"You're shocked," he says.

"You betcha. Jack, it's so beautiful."

I pull it out of the box and place it on my finger.

"I couldn't imagine starting the New Year without you as my fiancée. Will you marry me, Gwen? Will you be the Jill to this Jack?"

"This is so incredibly unexpected," I say, almost breathless.

"I know we have a lot to talk about."

My real excitement kicked in the next morning when I woke up and saw the ring on my finger, a dream that seemed to be living in my waking life. I watch Jack as he lies sleeping beside me, his hair a tousled mess—one leg sticking out from under the blankets—and I am in awe of what we might become together as Mr. and Mrs. Jack Madsen.

I saunter into the kitchen feeling like the only one who's ever worn a ring of promise on her finger, like Jack and I are members of an exclusive club. I rummage through the fridge for a bottle of champagne and the orange juice. I want to celebrate. When the cork hits the ceiling, I laugh as the spray from the bottle effervesces over my newly jeweled finger and I think all is delicious with the world. I dig through my fine-china cabinet for two crystal flutes and pour our breakfast toast.

We kiss and play our way through several rounds of mimosas with Christmas carols playing softly in the background and fall asleep again.

I allow myself the luxury of thinking about a wedding when we wake up. I will finally be able to say I have a husband. I am not going to be alone for the rest of my life. I understand now why he took on more work in the fall and had pushed himself a little more than normal. He wants to provide for us.

He tinkers around the house while I organize our meal in the kitchen. I am still getting used to seeing the diamond on my left ring finger.

I brought parts of my prepped menu from my work kitchen to my own kitchen. I want to do most of it at home. I am not afraid of a day in the kitchen on Christmas day. It is a festive way to spend my time. I stuff the chicken in slow-mo. I pick through the cranberries one by one—normally I grab small handfuls to not waste a moment, but this would be the most delicious meal I've ever made and I am not rushing it.

The garlic, the pine nuts, the chopped chives are taking on their own personality as they are dropped into my bowl of goat cheese. I add an extra chipotle pepper to the sauce I'll be using for the polenta and arugula. I want to taste the extreme smoky flavor and let my mouth burn with the new reality, and Jack likes spice. I fry off Georgina's polenta while the arugula wilts in the pan beside it. I arrange everything in my red ceramic ware so all I have to do is pop it into the oven when our guests arrive. I set the table, light the candles, and dream about a wedding I'll never forget but have given up hoping for.

Georgina hands me a giant poinsettia plant as she crosses the threshold. Philip comes in carrying a wine bottle in each hand. Georgina notices the ring on my finger immediately. "I like this guy. He has a good sense of the appropriate. It's been a nice amount of time already. You can tell he'll take care of things. Merry Christmas, Gwen.

"Look what Jack gave Gwen for Christmas," she says to Philip, pulling my hand forward. "Nice gift, isn't it?"

Jack winks at me.

"It beats candy canes and fruitcakes," Philip replies.

I lay the meal out on the table, our closest friends sitting around us. We toast our news, and then share stories of other proposals. One of Jack's friends is first.

"We were at a brunch and all of a sudden Ken got down on one knee. I backed up because I thought he wanted to pick up the crumbs that had fallen. He reached for my knees to keep me from going anywhere and pulled out a ring the size of an egg. Of course, I'm exaggerating but all I could do was say yes over and over again."

Ken stirs self-consciously in his chair and smiles bashfully.

"I know someone whose boyfriend proposed to her only after they'd nearly died in the Northridge earthquake," Genevieve says. "Walls were crumbling around him, foundations were shifting. The windows cracked. They were on the second of three floors. People were screaming. He thought they'd be crushed. The guy would never commit to her and she'd practically given up on him. And then a little tremor and the threat of loss of life and he antes up. They'd been seeing each other for years, and years."

We drain every bottle of wine. Jack goes to my study for more.

"I'd like to propose a toast to my future wife," he says.

His toast makes me feel so loved and hopeful for our future, I could never have guessed how tentative our future really is.

# Chapter Thirteen

## Van Buren-Gaines Divorce Party

Brunch Menu for 10

Three Cheese Fondue with Steamed Vegetables & Seared Cubes of Top Sirloin

Watercress Salad with Hearts of Palm, Tomato & Lemon Vinaigrette

Chocolate Fondue, Celebration Cake

I have a great love and a great life and yet something big is missing. Day in and day out I see us slipping apart. See! See! I try to warn Jack, but he isn't seeing it. Our interest in each other has waned. Our conversation has become drab, and uninspired. I don't feel honored or revered anymore.

He is standing in the doorway of the kitchen, coming toward me as he speaks, reaching for me, not stopping until he holds me. His embrace is love in its kindest and gentlest form. Its most silent as well, but his touch says more to me than words can ever evoke. I only hope he reads kindness in my response.

"I love you," he says, pulling me out of my hidden self. His words are so exposed I am caught off guard and, trying to find my way back to my center, wondering how he fits in. *Does he fit in? Or am I the one out of place?* He'd cut right through my heart.

*Do you love me?* didn't even need asking on his part. Love isn't the problem. Doubts have peppered our relationship for months and we don't seem to be able to get around them. We don't seem to have enough common ground. He is dear to my heart. In spite of everything, I want to kiss him.

I'm trying to make out some of the ingredients of this stew I'm in. I see physical attraction but a lack of unified vision bumping up against each other as they're stirred in the pot. And there's fear. Plain old fear in its purest form. Fear of what comes next if I walk away from this. Fear of life without my partner. Someone I've grown accustomed to.

We always think it's the stuff on the surface—the ingredients—that make the soup, but it's how it mingles and works together, the sum of all its parts, that gives it flavor.

What if I say yes to his marriage proposal and convince myself that so much of what I've been looking for comes with his offer? *What if* I follow this impulse and permit myself the desire to end it? Am I willing to live the lie another day? I skip breakfast with Jack and go straight to the kitchen, hoping my routine there will ground me.

Of all things, I need to start preparing for Shelly's wedding. I don't have the stomach for it today, as happy as I am for her. I delegate to Georgina who is in much better spirits, and thankfully, let me have my space. I sit in my office not knowing quite what to do.

I decide to call Patricia. Somehow it makes sense to reach out to her. She has a lot of time free now that she is on her way to divorce.

"Hello?" I can hear her voice.

Silence. I can't say a word. The tears come like a broken dam washing over me.

"Oh, sorry," I manage, trying to find my breath, "I didn't know I was going to cry. I guess I'll call you back."

I wait ten minutes and dial her again, regaining my composure enough to make the call.

"If it's like this now, it's going to be worse after you get married," Patricia says.

"Really?"

I didn't even have to tell her what was going on.

"Everything gets worse after you get married. You think you're tested now, just wait. Marriage is not for the faint of heart. Most women wouldn't make the decision to end it," she claims.

"Really? So, I'm smart? Is that what you're telling me? Because I don't feel so smart right now."

"Does he know?"

"Not outright, but he'd have to be in a coma to not have noticed something's off. I was just hoping my doubts would go away."

"But they're getting stronger instead."

"Yeah. There are other things getting in the way. Inconsistencies that weary me. I don't know what to do anymore."

"Sure, you do. Cry, cry, and cry. Then say goodbye to the pain and all the reasons why you forgot to be happy. Go to bed early and let tomorrow take care of itself."

It was good advice, but I can't bring myself to go home. I twiddle my thumbs over some of the details of Shelly's wedding instead. Then I rehash the whole thing with Georgina.

"Do you think he's happy?" she asks.

"I don't know for sure, but I think he's just playing it safe."

"Most men play it safe," she says. "Most men will stay in relationships they're not happy in rather than risk being alone. Are you happy?"

"I'm not unhappy. But no, I'm not really happy either. I just figured I was committed to this and we'd have to work it all out one way or another."

"You're more committed after the wedding. Believe me. I don't think happiness should be compromised. You have to start somewhere. Why should you stay if you're not happy? If you were already married, I'd have a different opinion."

Genevieve wasn't much help. She was so very opinionated. "So it's falling apart around you?" she asks.

"I guess I've got a lot of questions. The reality seems to have shifted somehow. I'm holding a giant *what if?* in my heart and hands. What if I was wrong about him? What if I follow this impulse to not marry him?"

"You haven't even set a date yet. You don't have to get ahead of yourself. It's good to make sure this is what you want before it's too late. He's a good guy, but some men make better boyfriends than they do husbands. I think if you go through with this, you're just lying to justify a decision you aren't comfortable making."

"Wow. Okay."

I don't know the answers, but I am willing to live the lie another day while I figure it all out. Suddenly I know why so many people stay together after the love is gone. It's denial that the love is gone. There must be such comfort in believing in the status quo. If not, addresses will change, morning habits will change, lifetime guarantees will change. I'll be left with myself, and what kind of ending is that?

*!!***!!***!!*

WHEN HE comes home, I want to kiss him—to take him into my arms and dance around the kitchen cheek to cheek, humming my ummings and yummings with glazed eyes and pursed lips, pretending everything is okay. I decide to keep positive and try to ignore what I don't like. There's still plenty of time to fix it.

In no time at all, I realize the path of least resistance is overcrowded.

*!!***!!***!!*

I HEAR from Allison Gaines at the end of the day. She and Shelly will be sisters-in-law soon. I nearly let the call go to voice mail, but I'd done so little all day, I feel obliged to answer. I recognize her voice immediately.

"I have a request. I'm not even sure you do this sort of thing, but would you cater my divorce?"

"Divorce! What divorce? I thought you were happy." I am immediately speaking in a high-pitched voice. "Does Shelly know? She thinks you and Brian are still living in wedded bliss after all these years. I'm working on her wedding, you know. As we speak."

"Well, Shelly's sweet, but not really on top of things, and I haven't bothered her with the details. She has enough to think about with her wedding coming up so soon. And I don't want to jinx her."

"Well, you're jinxing me." Truthfully, I'd already jinxed myself plenty.

"We're not even divorced yet officially, but I know you're busy and I wanted to make sure you would do it—that's if you even do divorce parties—when the time comes. We filed months and months ago and it's about as friendly a divorce as one could hope for, and an inevitable end I'm afraid. I've been bored for years. I've certainly put up a good front, so when the time comes, I really want to celebrate my new freedom."

"Where would you want to have it—not at your house?"

"If our timing is right, I'll be closing escrow on a hip little townhouse in Studio City a few weeks before the divorce is final, and I'll have just enough time to do some painting and move in."

"Are you sure you don't want to just have a housewarming party then? Perhaps it would be in better taste."

"No. I really want to celebrate our end. The middle was so long and drawn out."

I can't help but see some similarities between Jack and me.

"Have you thought about the menu and what you might want to serve? Is this a daytime thing or an evening thing?" I find it hard to take her seriously, but my practical business sense is innate and unstoppable.

"I was thinking a Saturday afternoon would work well. Maybe fondue or something light. Maybe some cocktails. It's just going to be my closest girlfriends—the ones who have watched our painful charade this whole time and gone the distance with me. I think they're as relieved as I am. I was thinking something flambéed for dessert—like maybe cherries jubilee—doesn't that get set on fire? I'd like to burn our marriage certificate ceremoniously. Brian said I could have it. He's keeping the house after all."

"Allison, are you pulling my leg?" This just isn't adding up for me. Not today. "I mean—I adore you, but this just seems to be a little out of character and while I'm trying to take you seriously, I'm really in shock."

"I'm quite serious. I'm just trying to make the most of a bad situation."

"That I understand. Why don't we talk in a few days? Let me mull all this over and I'll call you with some ideas." It is all the professionalism I could muster.

I really am in shock—and I still have to go home and face Jack. Hearing Allison talk helps me seal my own fate. By focusing on the positive I might have talked myself into a few more years with Jack—at least—but the stakes will be higher by then. My friends will call it the Devine denial. I do want more out of love, certainly more out of a marriage. *Say yes, it's true.* He is not the one for me. He is the road—another is my destination.

When I really feel into my heart, my gut, when I feel into these deepest parts of myself, I know I can't go through with it. I cannot marry without the passion and the in-love part while questioning the whole foundation, just because I'm not ready to face single life. I don't want to put myself out there again. Right in the midst of planning a wedding I have to face the fact that I can't face the marriage. Oh, what heartbreak! What a letdown!

I don't know what to do with this truth. It is tempting to let this go on forever.

*!!***!!***!!*

"HI, JACK, I'm home," I call from the doorway, half hoping he's out.

"In here."

I walk toward the back room, somber in mood, determined in intention. I start before I can stop myself. "Listen, I've been doing some thinking and I want to call off the engagement. I just don't think it's a good thing for either of us. Something's missing. I think you feel it, too, and I just don't believe in planning for a future with you unless I'm in it wholeheartedly. I get the feeling sometimes you're not even sure and you're just going through the motions and I don't believe a marriage should be built on that. I've wanted to be married for so long and maybe my idealistic thoughts are getting in the way, but I just can't shake this feeling we're making a terrible mistake. You know it. I know it. There doesn't seem to be much effort to work it out and that's not good for a marriage in the long run and I know somehow you agree with me, but haven't been willing to see it or maybe you have seen it, but haven't been willing to accept it. I don't know." I can't seem to stop talking and then he makes me stop. Literally. He puts his hand over my mouth.

"I know we're lost, Gwen. I've been trying to work it out in my head as well. I love you so much and you're right, it's not working, is it? I was just hoping something would break and we'd be able to change our ways."

Here it is, the coldhearted truth that we aren't a we. I admit I'd tried to talk myself into this all along. Convincing myself that so much of what I've been looking for was offered by him.

We sleep in spooned positions for most of the night, comforting each other, holding on, not desperately, but with the certainty that we are over, recognizing that our love for each other isn't enough. We wake and something I'd forgotten stirs in me. I reach for him. Kiss him and let him kiss me back. Exploring each other with a recognition I know will comfort me later. And then he's inside me and I remember who we are. There is still love and I can dance this liquid dance and let it move me. He stops, pulls himself away from me, taking my breath with him. He lies there and I feel tears on my flesh. His tears. All this time together and I had no idea he can cry.

I feel my heart break into a thousand different pieces then, but it is his heart I hold in my hands tenderly. Then my tears are falling on us both, wishing they could rinse away this bittersweet reality and return it to its hopeful place. I think about the gods and their work in all of this. How they'd orchestrated our participation. How they'd made us believe we'd be together. Believe we did, with all our hearts.

*Here we go again, Gwen. When, Gwen, would you get it right?* I feel like I'm nearing my shelf life.

*!!***!!***!!*

I GATHERED my wits enough to call Allison back and make menu suggestions for her divorce party.

"Well, Allison, I do like your idea of fondue," I say into the phone. "It's both savory and light and I was going to suggest doing a three-cheese fondue with Emmentaler, sharp cheddar, and fontina. I think the flavors will blend nicely. I was thinking steamed broccoli, red pepper, strips of smoked chicken, green grapes, and apples for dipping. How does that sound to you?"

"I really like it. Can we do a salad as well?"

"Sure. Why not a watercress salad with chopped tomato, toasted pine nuts, hearts of palm with a really light lemon vinaigrette? It would be a great complement to the fondue. And it's not a salad you see very often."

"See, there's a reason Shelly and I like you to do everything for us. You're so good at bringing it all together."

"I want to talk you out of this cherries jubilee idea. I think burning the marriage certificate is fire enough. I don't want to see desserts on fire. Especially if you're doing this in a newly painted dining room."

"Okay, I'll concede you're right."

"I'd rather do my celebration cake for you. I make it myself. It's a sponge cake with custard and seasonal berry filling. It's iced with whipped cream and decorated with more fresh berries. It's a great cake to have champagne with and I think it'll round out the menu nicely."

"Genius. Delicious. Let's do it."

"So how are things coming along anyway? Are we close to a date? One I can put on the calendar?"

"Yes, let's do it the second Saturday of next month. I think that's plenty of time to get settled at my new place and I know the divorce will be final by then."

I spend what's left of my day speed dialing my girlfriends to let them know my decision about Jack. This is not something I keep under wraps. I have to talk, have to get it out. Repetitive as it is, I have to keep hearing myself say it so I can accept what I've been trying to for weeks and months.

"I'm thinking he was never meant to be my husband," I tell Georgina. "Maybe I'm wrong and with a little shift in perspective there is a future here, but I don't see our children. I can't imagine them ever coming into this world through my body and breathing their own lives. I can't imagine how we'd ever get that far."

"Better to see incompatibilities sooner rather than later."

"I guess I just expected more," I say.

Genevieve's response doesn't make me feel any better at all. "It's probably your last chance."

"Gee, thanks."

"Really. The older you get the harder it is to find someone. After forty, your life goes down the drain. If I were you, I wouldn't pass it up. No one's going to want you."

"Genevieve! That's a terrible thing to say."

"I know. You're right, but I'm still mad about Hermie. That bird was my everything. Maybe it will be better if you get married. Maybe he'll work on the relationship then—take it more seriously. I lived with two confirmed bachelors once. They were older too. Age does something to you. They would never get married. There are some men who just aren't going there. At least Jack was willing to go there."

She makes me doubt why I need to end this.

"You won't meet anyone else. If you do, you're lucky."

I am in a total state of confusion when we hang up. Maybe I won't know a good thing if it bites me in the behind.

*!!***!!***!!*

ONCE I am home, I raid my clear jars of candy and snacks and delectable gourmet treats. I expected Jack and me to have a common ground that would not waver, but I can't figure out what ground I'm standing on. I'm not twenty-one anymore. I'm wiser now and I've been around the block. I find the definitive, unwavering parts of myself and am aghast to see them mirrored in the man I hoped would be beside me. I expected to accept flawed characteristics in both of us, and still be together. I didn't expect to come this far and end up alone. We'd both mourned the end of this relationship already. We agreed we were doing the right thing by ending it now. I had to admit how much Jack had helped me grow—way beyond the resentments Robert helped me create.

*!!***!!***!!*

THE DISHES are never-ending or so it seems. I find myself at the sink washing, washing, washing. I want to keep busy at any cost to keep my mind from working through the reasons I walked away. It was so important at the time, but now I can't remember my reasons.

Georgina helps to reduce any amount of effort on my part to run the kitchen while I mend my wounded heart. She is doing a great job taking care of the daily mundane chores. She lets me get away with washing the dishes and makes some of the decisions without me. She is probably trying her best to stave off the onset of my impending breakdown should something go wrong.

She hasn't asked me a thing about the breakup, but I notice she's done a thorough job in removing Jack's presence from the kitchen. She has done it quietly and efficiently. The long-form plastic apron he bought me a few months ago wasn't hanging beside the deep fryer anymore. The magnets with his face on them weren't hanging on the fridge where we kept our prep lists either. Even the Italian rock-salt-and-pepper set he'd given me is gone from its place on the spice rack above one of our workstations. In its place is another set I'd seen at Gelson's last week. I wonder what she's done with everything but don't bother to ask.

This breakup is even harder because I chose it willingly. Love itself is deceiving and malleable. It comes and goes like the passing of the day. The heart can be so divided. It can love and not love all at the same time.

*!!***!!***!!*

GEORGINA IS working pretty closely with Shelly on the décor package for her wedding, so I have to debrief Georgina regarding the confidentiality of Allison's divorce party. It is important Shelly doesn't know about it before her wedding day. Allison has jinxed enough already. Georgina, however, is really coming into her own. I see she'll need a raise soon. My profits are increasing with her work and it is only fair I pass a share of it along to her. I want her to be more prepared to handle things on her own if things don't work out with Philip. Suddenly I am planning for both our futures. I haven't heard much from her about how things are going with him. It's probably her way of respecting my mourning period and not rubbing my face in her happiness. I am happy for her regardless, and I do appreciate her discretion.

The day has come to put Allison's divorce party together. I am thankful for such an easy party to prepare. Georgina is coming with me to set up and staying until the end.

Allison's new place is on Woodbridge, tucked away at the end of a dead-end street, which I hope doesn't forebode where her love life is going now that the divorce is final. It's a pretty little building with a separate entrance for each unit instead of a common entry. She's done a great job with the painting and it is very much a girl's place—the homogenous decorating style of her house with Brian was not even remotely carried over here. It is clear she's begun a new life and it looks good on her. I can feel my own psyche expanding and relaxing in a way I haven't felt since my split with Jack.

Her friends arrive, dressed casually, some in jeans, others in stretch pants like they've come straight from yoga class. It's the first time they've seen the place, too, and I can tell Allison wants her new life to be unveiled all at once, with an audience commending her efforts.

"Brian who?" she says with rosy cheeks and glittering eyes, if anyone asks how he was or how she is doing without him. "This is how I'm doing without him," she says, her arm reaching out to present her new surroundings.

She is doing well enough from what I can see. I helped Georgina pour them their first glasses of wine and set up the fondue dishes. We set everything up on a large coffee table and arrange oversized pillows so everyone can sit comfortably on the floor. It reminds me of a slumber party without the pajamas and overnight stay. When the platters of ingredients are set out and the candles are lit under the cheese-filled fondue dishes, I make my exit. Georgina is tossing the salad when I say my goodbyes to her, and then to Allison.

"Well, you've done it again, Gwen. Thanks so much." She gives me a hug and a kiss that smells lightly of the crisp chardonnay we chose to complement her menu and I was happy for her and, oddly, happy for myself too. She is infectious. I feel as free as Allison is bragging to be. And I feel hopeful.

*!!***!!***!!*

I MISS us throughout the day, every day, but I never waver in believing it isn't meant to be—even with Genevieve's doomed opinion still looming in my thoughts. I have no regrets. I showed up. I gave it my best. Next time, I am going to get it right.

# Chapter Fourteen

## Philip's Promotion Party

Menu for 25

Caprese Salad, Avocado & Mandarin Salad
Salt Crusted Steak, Southern Fried Chicken
Herb Roasted Vegetables, Rosemary Garlic Mashed Potatoes
Gourmet Snowballs, Apple Cobbler

Georgina invites me over for a small party she and Philip are hosting in honor of Philip's recent promotion. It is something they both have been hoping for and want to celebrate with a small group of close friends.

"I'm still hoping for a ring. Maybe once his raise kicks in," she admits.

"What would you like me to bring?"

She shrugs. "I've got it covered."

"You know I don't like to show up empty-handed. It makes me nervous. I'll bring some flowers for your table."

By the time I show up, with a large bouquet of purple irises and yellow tulips, there are several guests in her kitchen arranging platters and bowls of food they brought.

"You didn't tell me this was potluck," I say into her ear as I hand her the flowers.

"You wouldn't have come."

"Oh, I'm not that much of a snob." My hands are already sweating though.

"Sure, you're not, but the color has practically drained out of your face. If I mentioned potluck, you'd have made a four-course meal and brought it in the Cambro to keep it warm until we were ready to serve. Or you'd have had other plans. Tell me I'm wrong. You don't have to worry. I've got everything covered."

"All right, all right, take your flowers."

"Thank you so much. It was thoughtful of you to not come empty-handed."

Potluck. More like crapshoot. If you're lucky you like it. If you have no taste, you love it. I've never seen a potluck that was well planned. Usually the portions are way off too. There is always too much of one thing and not enough of another, and it all looks sloppy when displayed.

Someone invariably brings potato chips and puts them in a bowl in the middle of the table. Then you find chips in your fruit salad later—a fruit salad with grapes that have seeds, and orange chunks with sloppy pieces of rind still sticking to them. None of that goes well with the three versions of potato salad flanking it on every side. I always want to bring order to the food display before I can actually make it through dinner.

Georgina is right. If she let me know this would be a potluck I would not have come. It is possible I'll be leaving right after the drink I'm determined to get. "You're worrying for nothing. Go have a drink," she says.

"Where's the bar set up?"

"In the alcove under the stairway. Philip's making margaritas right now. Hurry over. And once you've had one, have another."

Friends of theirs are milling about with drinks in hand and they seem to know one another quite well. Once I get my first margarita down, I decide to brave helping Georgina in the kitchen.

"What are those?" I ask, pointing to mounds of a white cake-like substance.

"Oh, those are Rosie's gourmet version of snowballs. They're truly amazing."

"And that?" I ask, pointing again.

"That's Sam's apple cobbler."

"Okay, so you've got dessert covered. That actually looks pretty good."

Now that I've had a good look at everything, it really isn't all that bad. Georgina has enough sense to make a pretty presentation out of it all. She moves some of the food to her own set of dishes, so it all has an appealing theme and my flowers give the table the right pack of punch. There is a caprese salad with fresh bread beside it, and a green salad with large wedges of avocado and mandarin slices, and I am really happy to note, no potato salad.

I begin to relax, and my second margarita isn't half bad either.

I stop worrying about the food and take in the crowd. I notice Philip talking and laughing with a good-looking man in the corner near the bar. They are laughing so much I actually feel left out. His laugh is warm and inviting, it draws me in from all the way across the room. He is tall, dark, and handsome in an understated way. Sports jacket and black jeans. Shiny belt buckle. I am a voyeur, he is my guilty pleasure. Twinkle, twinkle lots of stars when he catches me watching him, our eyes lock in unison, a blush climbs my cheeks. He looks right through me. I feel champagne bubbles in my stomach even though tequila is lacing my veins.

"Who's that with Philip?" I ask Georgina.

"Oh, that's Reuben."

"As in the sandwich?"

"Yes, I hear he's quite a mouthful."

Now I am laughing.

"He made an amazing medley of roasted vegetables with fresh herbs. It's in the oven right now. He's a good cook. Philip and he have been friends since their school days. Really nice guy. I never really thought of it before, but you'd probably be good together."

"Why do you think so?"

"Well, he's just very thoughtful."

"How so?"

"One time he stayed with us and wanted to heat up spaghetti and meatball leftovers in the microwave. He put a plate over the bowl so it didn't spray sauce all over the insides, and he washed the dishes before going to bed rather than leaving them all gross in the sink for us to do the next day."

"That is thoughtful."

"And efficient."

"Yeah, but will he eat pie for breakfast?"

"Go ask him."

"I'm not that curious."

"Yeah. Sure."

We finish making pretty with the food. Rosie comes over, looks at everything longingly. "I wore tight jeans today so every time I eat, I'll have something to think about. If I eat chocolate, I break out in fat. This all looks so good, it's going to hurt later," she says.

"Is this the kind of party where people get loaded and go home with each other?" I wonder, hungry for a Reuben sandwich.

Georgina ignores me and calls dinner—actually announces it with a dinner bell that can be heard above the music playing in the living room. Guests start making their way toward the kitchen. She advises me, "If you fill anyone else's plate but your own, I'm sending you home. Immediately."

I fill my own plate only and take a seat at the dining table. I never did like buffet style where you have to balance a plate on your thigh—it makes the whole meal feel too casual. Reuben sits down beside me. I start to get nervous. I feel self-conscious and awkward.

I have food in my mouth he doesn't need to see, so I just nod when he says hello, my lips curl to form a smile, despite my chewing. He has a neat arrangement of food on his plate, a napkin on his lap, his fork in the proper hand, and he doesn't lick his knife once throughout the whole meal.

"I'm a friend of Philip's," he manages to say without showing me the contents of his mouth, for which I am deeply grateful—and he says this after I have a chance to swallow my own food. I like his manners.

"I'm a friend of Georgina's. We work together."

"The catering company?"

"Yes. Your vegetables are delicious. Nice touch with the mint and tarragon. Good combination of flavors."

"Thanks. I love to cook. I was thinking I might want to open a restaurant one day. It runs in my family."

"With a name like Reuben you should open a deli."

"Yeah, it is my birthright. My grandfather invented the Reuben."

"Seriously? You're practically a celebrity."

"Well, the sandwich is for sure. I'm just his offspring."

"There's a lot of folklore around the Reuben. Some think it was invented in Nebraska."

"New York born and raised. Named after my dad. With a claim to fame like that the name stuck."

"How do you make it?"

"I can't tell you that."

"Family secret?"

"Yeah. Locked in the vault family secret. Lineups around the block secret. You must have some secrets yourself."

"The secret is in the sauce."

"My grandpops used to say that."

"That's my line."

So, we talk, and talk, and talk. He leaves the table long enough to bring us both back a plate of gourmet snowballs. Surprisingly, they are truly amazing, as Georgina had promised, and a perfect end to the meal.

He produces a handful of toothpicks and offers me one.

"Thanks. I'm good." There is no way I am picking my teeth in front of him.

"They're cinnamon. I just like to suck on them."

"Where on earth do you get cinnamon toothpicks?"

"They're imported. I'm a food distributor."

I took one after all.

I'd sorted through enough men already to know a good egg when I saw one. I couldn't have seen this coming for all my wanting, hoping, and dreaming. I'd die and go to heaven if he happens to like me enough to ask me out. But I am not going to wait around and find out. I excuse myself and tell him I am leaving.

"It was nice meeting you, Reuben," I say, extending my hand.

He stands up immediately and follows me while I say my goodbyes to Georgina and Philip.

"Thanks, Georgina, for inviting me. I had a great time. Really delicious dinner too. Philip, congratulations again."

"Here, I'll walk you to your car," Reuben says quietly, and I turn beet red instantly under the watchful eye of Georgina.

"Well, can I call you sometime?" he asks once I am seated in my car, the window rolled down so we can talk.

"Sure. Here's my card," I say, but I fumble with it and it floats to the ground instead of into his hand. By the time he picks it up I am lurching forward in my car, nervously. I am afraid he'll kiss me—and hoping that he does. I wave through my open window. "Well, bye for now."

*!!***!!***!!*

"Do you like him?" Georgina asks on Monday, barely through the door of the kitchen before the words are out of her mouth.

"Yeah, I like him."

"But do you like him, like him?" Georgina is persistent today. "Really, really, like him?"

"What is this, high school?"

"Well?"

"Yes, I do."

"I knew you'd like him, like him."

"But do you think he likes me likes me?" We giggle, but not too indulgently. Neither of us wants to jinx this. Whatever this is.

"Did he ask you out?"

"Yeah."

"Ooh, I knew it. You're going to marry him you know. This is the guy for you. I can't believe I didn't think of it myself. You're perfect for each other. I know you, and I know him, and I know I'm right. You're going to marry him. Even Philip thinks so."

*!!***!!***!!*

I THINK about Reuben for days, hoping I hear from him again, and again, and then some. If he is anything like the sandwich, he will be multidimensional, with layers of beautiful complexities and he'll stand the test of time. When I do hear from him, he suggests a picnic lunch and is determined to bring it to my kitchen of all places. "Let's eat together. I'll bring you some goodies. What time can you step away from your kitchen?"

"Anytime, but my hunger kicks in at around one P.M."

He shows up on time, a picnic basket in one hand and a box in the other. He passes me the box and kisses me on the cheek. Georgina and he exchange small talk while I rummage through the contents. Bocconcini in olive oil and herbs, roasted red peppers, sun-dried tomatoes, mascarpone cheese, plump tomatoes under glass. Elephant garlic and oversized basil. He makes me want to break out in bruschetta. He brought olives I never knew existed. I am going to need a minute to soak this all in. I hide in the bathroom and stare in the mirror long enough to really see myself. The logical thing to do is to take a step forward. He is meeting me more than halfway.

He is waiting for me when I reappear. I hug him and thank him for the box. I barely notice his hand on my apron strings. He pulls and lifts and before you know it my lip-blotched apron is our tablecloth. He lays it out on the tailgate of his pickup truck and is reaching for the basket's contents. I watch his hands and want them on me. Out comes breaded chicken fillets on fresh kaisers and cold pasta salad. An heirloom tomato and cucumber salad with tangy red vinegar with fresh-cut chives follows. We eat in the parking lot out back under the sun and smog. It makes me feel like

I am on holiday and yet my busy world is just a few steps away. Georgina peeks out the kitchen window occasionally.

"So, what's your deal?" I want to know. "Are you the love 'em and leave 'em type?"

"No, I'm the love 'em and love 'em some more type."

"In that case," I say, because I need to know, "what are you planning to do with me? I'm asking because I—"

"I'm going to squeeze you like an orange," he replies.

I laugh out loud, joyfully, guiltily.

Then he says, "I'm going to lick you like a lollipop, make you sizzle like a steak, and cream you like corn."

"Is that all in one sitting?" I ask, and I know we are speaking the same language. I know he gets me.

"Yup," he replies with confidence.

"Well, there's plenty of lip service in your future then."

Smiles on both our faces.

And so we begin—and he cooks for me too. All kinds of things—he is a wizard with flash in the pan cooking. He knows how to make something out of nothing in no time flat. He makes it look as good as it tastes. It is clear he likes to do it—his talent for it comes from his inner sensibilities and his desire for perfection. Yet he lives beyond the veneer of perfection in his own perfectly imperfect world and I know I can slip into it comfortably without missing any of myself. He cleans up after himself, too, just as Georgina has implied.

"What's your favorite ice cream?" I ask him once. "Just so I know."

"Well, it isn't rocky road. There's too much stuff in the way of the chocolate. I prefer plain and simple deep dark chocolate. But I wouldn't settle for just any chocolate. Haagen Dazs is my one true favorite."

He has clear skin and a smooth complexion he attributes to the three cloves of garlic he eats religiously every day, and the raw onion he adds to his salads. Somehow, he doesn't taste like garlic or onions, which wins my immediate respect.

*!!***!!***!!*

I NEARLY gasp when he shows me his herb garden—a virtual feast for my senses. The first time he takes me out there I can't even touch his basil or his rosemary, tempted as I am by all of it. His sage is impressive too. It isn't until I see it for the second time that I allow myself to reach tentatively with my nose and then my hands, dragging them across the velvety leaves to let their aroma settle into me, the dew still clinging to their parts.

He has a small pair of clippers he uses to cut off pieces—letting the scent really fill the air—and he brushes the chocolate mint across my tongue so I taste it. Then he rubs the chocolate mint leaves along my bare shoulder and comes in close.

"There, now I can taste this on you later."

We don't get out of the garden. Later will never come we are so stuck in the moment. He takes me like he owns me, without doubt. Without reserve. I smell the rosemary and sage. My knees are in peppermint, my elbows in thyme.

He wasn't kidding when he said he'd cream me like corn. He opened my husk and spilt the contents. I am oozing from every self-inflicted border. He is breaking down my defenses. He makes safe a special place. I surrender my resistances and all my doubts. I get comfortable on a bed of lemon thyme. He is lost under my skirt, all mouth, all hands, all encompassing.

He mutters, "You're divine, Ms. Devine." Our bodies fit like they were made from all our missing parts, finally together after too long without each other. We tumble and curl around each other, his own scent evocative, his presence undaunting. He has complete command over all my orgasms. I want him inside me until the end of time.

I come to rely on him and even need him. I need to wake up throughout the night and know that some part of us is touching. An arm around a waist, hands intertwined, a face against a shoulder, knee to knee. The touch and feel of skin on skin. It transmits safety and a sense of wholeness. These are the little things that make me happy, the little things that make the picture complete for me.

My world becomes small. It is just he and I. The you and me of love's defined moments. We are an item. My friends fall to the wayside. He is my dream, my inspiration.

"Reuben, I want to make you pancakes for breakfast," I say dreamily as we lie there, upside down in bed, hand in hand, still basking in each other.

"I love pancakes."

"I have a secret recipe I've never shared with anyone. They may be the best pancakes you've ever tasted."

"A lot of what you do is the best I've ever tasted," he replies with sass.

"Well, let's get a move on."

I stand in the kitchen measuring my milk and eggs and flour, humming softly to myself, while he rummages in the refrigerator for orange juice and cream for his coffee.

"You were a composite before you showed up," I tell him. "I'd seen bits and pieces of you all along, maybe that's why I never let myself settle with anyone else. Because I was a work in progress, simmering in the stew of my own mistakes. You've taken the mystery out of me. All the years men couldn't figure out what to do with me are gone like they didn't exist."

"And do you want to get married?" he asks, then, "That's not a proposal, that's just a question. I was just wondering what you want."

"I want the whole mashed potato. It's true I've always had the dream of a successful marriage. I just didn't dare to dream it alive. I held my breath. I've been holding it for years. Now I know why I had so many unavailable men. So I could blame them instead of myself, the real and guilty culprit. Should I try and fail, I would be crushed ice in a melting puddle."

"It's great to be in love, isn't it?" he says, out of nowhere. Not that I am not feeling the in-love part, I just didn't expect him to mention it.

"Yes. To think I'm in love with a man who is in love with me."

"That's better than pancakes any day."

We are in bed again before the syrup dries on our plates.

# Chapter Fifteen

## Gaines/Van Buren Wedding

Menu for 150
Santa Fe Salad with Apple Chili Dressing
Marinated Top Round Sirloin
El Paso Chicken
Carrot & Cauliflower Sauté

Shelly is a nervous wreck now that her wedding is less than a week away. Adam is such a catch, I am sure she has nothing to worry about, but she is outright suffering from pre-wedding jitters. She sets the little door chime off when she opens the door to the Lip Service kitchen and it keeps ringing and ringing. It's like she brought the energy right in with her. I can almost see her hair shaking. She is a full fifteen minutes early.

Georgina has just started gathering the spices I use in my Tex-Mex spice blend. I use it in a bunch of great tasting recipes including my El Paso chicken. We are going to make a big batch. I need it in two of Shelly's menu items. I want to move through our to-do list quickly. So much for that. I let Georgina start without me and lead Shelly to my office. I have to spend a lot of time reassuring her instead.

"He loves you. He adores you. He proposed to you. Men just don't propose every day. Believe me. You're fine."

"I'm just afraid I'll fall short of what he expects from a wife."

"Don't be silly. You're his best friend. He loves you deeply. He's waited so long for this. Haven't you known each other since college?"

"Yeah. We're both from El Paso."

"You were practically made for each other, I think. This isn't frivolous. I've seen the way he looks at you."

"Okay. My final count for RSVPs is 150. We wanted it to feel more intimate, but it turns out some of our Texan relatives are coming in after all. I hope I don't regret having the reception at the country club in Brentwood." She sounds doubtful.

"I don't know why you would. It's so beautiful. The staff is incredible too."

"You're right. You're right about everything. I feel better."

I am not convinced she's convinced, but at least she isn't breathing in short, shallow breaths anymore. We finalize what we can. I don't want to overwhelm her or activate her insecurities any further. I watch her as she leaves, hoping it is safe to let her loose on the world.

I rejoin Georgina in the kitchen. "I hope Shelly doesn't bolt the day of her wedding—if she even makes it that far, she's so nervous."

"She looks a little pale," Georgina says. "She didn't even say goodbye. What if she chickens out?"

"I'm going to think of her every time I make El Paso chicken and have already dubbed her the El Paso Chicken for sure. It might very well ruin the future of this recipe. I'd hate to see that happen to Adam."

"What is El Paso chicken by the way?" Georgina asks.

"A fancy name for a southwestern dish I make using my Tex-Mex rub. I mix bread and cake crumbs in with dried chilis, paprika, garlic, and some other spices. The spices tenderize it and the bread crumbs lock in the moisture so the chicken is zesty and succulent."

"That sounds like something I'd like to eat right now."

"The tomatoes and onions are sautéed in butter until soft and then puréed in the Cuisinart and reheated. The carrots and cauliflower florets are simmered in just enough sauce to make the vegetables flavorful without being messy. I usually steam them partially before adding them to the tomato and onion mixture. Keeps the sauce from drying out while waiting for the cauliflower and carrots to cook to tender. The top round is marinated in slivered garlic, soy sauce, and some herbs. There's something else I usually put in it, but I've gone blank. I can't remember. Oh, well, we have a few days yet. It'll come back to me. The rice is a cinch. We'll cube roasted poblano chilis and some roasted red pepper and add that like confetti as the last step and the meal will be beautiful, as will their life together."

"I don't remember who I booked to serve. Let me dig into my file here." Georgina is not disorganized so she finds the list easily.

"Let's call Chef Mate and confirm no one's forgotten about us."

"We have two of their guys booked. One handling appetizers, the other the main course."

*!!***!!***!!*

I'VE JUST returned from work and hear Reuben clanking around in my kitchen. It isn't the first time he's let himself in to surprise me with a home-cooked meal. He is smart enough to know I don't always want to cook when I get home.

"Hi, Little Miss Muffet."

"Hello, Mr. Potato Head."

"I just made a salad to stop a herd of rhinos."

"That sounds serious. What's in it?"

"All things green and nutritious. You've got to do the dressing. You know me, I only know how to pour from bottles. I don't know the first thing about making a dressing from scratch."

He pulls at the zipper of my skirt.

"Hey. I'm trying to do the dressing."

"And I'm trying to do the undressing."

To make love to him is a deliciously intoxicating experience. He makes me scream food expletives loudly in his darkened bedroom. Pillow talk and dark talk and whispered silences that speak so much. I am unattached to the outcome. Finally, simply, able to love just for love's sake.

*!!***!!***!!*

SHELLY WANTS cuttings from a pepper tree and sunflowers as center pieces on the tables. I think it's an odd combination until I see the arrangement the florist has come up with. It is striking against the blue tablecloths.

She wears a Vera Wang dress that is sculpted to her body and accentuates her delicate features. Everything about her is streamlined. She isn't a mess of extra fabric—she is sleek and classy. She is still very nervous, but her sisters and friends hover closely, keeping the conversation light and telling her she looks beautiful.

Adam wears a chocolate brown tuxedo that accentuates his trim physique and sun-bleached hair. He stands waiting for her out at the altar, confident, a smile in his eyes. He is smiling from the inside out.

Even though I am catering the event, she's insisted I be a guest at her wedding ceremony, and she expects me to bring a guest. The time I spend making sure my staff knows what they are doing so I can attend is well worth it. With Georgina managing them, I am confident things will go well. And with Reuben at my side, I am completely happy.

It is intriguing to see Shelly advance toward Adam at the altar, the distance closing between them, all their friends and family surrounding them with love and hope and inspired grace. I see Shelly has lost her nervousness in favor of her faith in her love for Adam, finally seeing she has nothing to worry about at all. He has chosen her as she has him. The words of the priest are lost to me as I bask in the dreaminess of love and recognize my own for Reuben and his for me.

I lean into him in the pew.

"I love you more than dinner," I reveal to him. It is true. I do. I do love him more than dinner. My dinner, his dinner, the dinner I prepared for everyone that day. I am a lucky girl.

The ceremony ends and we made the short walk over to the reception hall, stopping to kiss under a jacaranda tree, its lavender-colored flowers bulging everywhere.

He's down on one knee in a flash. "Will you marry me?" he asks.

Four words. I expected more. And I got it. So much meaning and yet so easy to understand what he means by them, I know him so well. I did want to marry him. All this time I'd secretly scoffed at marriage like I was too good for the sacrament, all the while missing the whole point. To share and share alike. To be wholly one and one to make two.

I see the way he looks at me when he thinks I am not paying attention. He adores me. He craves me like the sweetest treat in heaven. I know this and trust this. I know we'll be together and that every day that follows this one will have him in it.

I can hardly refuse. Some things just make sense. I can have my cake and share it too. I want a private ceremony—just me and him and a few of our people to make it real. He pulls the ring from his pocket, and slips it on my finger, a perfect fit. A ring he claims was made for me, a myriad of little diamonds fit together in a large cluster that glistens and shines in the sun. "Each of these diamonds represents all the years I plan on loving you."

I remember eating my dinner. Delicious. The rest of the evening is a blur.

*!!***!!***!!*

# Quickies and One-Bite Stands

## Gwen's Free-Range Eggs

1–2 tbsp. butter
6 large eggs
2 cups of fresh spinach leaves, cleaned and dried
2 tbsp. chèvre
Pinch of salt and pepper

Talk about an easy egg dish, and ready in a flash. Generously butter the cups of a nonstick muffin tin. Line with spinach leaves in an overlapping layered way to create a nest for the eggs. Crack the eggs separately one at a time, without breaking the yolks, and add one to each of the cups. Add a pinch of salt and pepper to each. Bake in a 300-degree oven until the eggs set. Add equal amounts of chèvre to each cup and continue to bake until the chèvre melts and the egg whites are opaque.

# Custard French Toast with Warm Blueberry Compote

French Toast Batter

6 eggs
2 tbsp. sugar
¼ tsp. salt
¼ tsp. nutmeg
¼ tsp. cinnamon
½ cup flour
2 cups whole milk
loaf of french bread, sliced
butter

Use an electric beater to blend eggs with sugar, salt, and spices. Add half the flour and milk at a time until well blended (no lumps). Slice the french bread and put into a glass oblong dish or cookie sheet with sides. Pour the batter over the bread to soak it.

Use a skillet with a matching lid. Heat it on medium-high. Add butter to the pan so it melts without burning and add enough slices to fill the pan. Cook until golden, then turn the heat down to medium. Add more butter to the pan as you flip the slices. Lower heat to medium-low, add the lid, and continue to cook until golden brown. Serve with warm blueberry compote, drizzle with maple syrup, and top with whipped cream.

# Warm Blueberry Compote

2 pints fresh blueberries
1 tbsp. quick-cooking tapioca
2 tbsp. cane sugar
1 tsp. cinnamon
¼ tsp. salt
½ tsp. lemon rind or 1 squeeze of lemon juice (optional)

Clean and rinse blueberries and add to a nonstick pot or pan. Add tapioca pearls, cinnamon, and salt and coat the blueberries. Allow to rest for five minutes. Cook on medium heat until the blueberries start to boil and their liquid starts to thicken. Reduce immediately to the lowest low, put a lid on, and keep warm until ready to serve. Do not overcook. Compote will thicken as it cools.

# Honey Citrus Chicken

HONEY CITRUS MARINADE

2 cups honey
⅓ cup orange juice
⅓ cup lime juice
⅓ cup lemon juice
1 tsp. salt
2 cloves garlic minced

This is enough to marinate 6–8 chicken breasts.

Add all ingredients to a large bowl, stir until mixed. Pour over cleaned, thawed chicken breasts and marinate overnight. When ready to cook, drain chicken and discard the marinade. Add one tablespoon oil to pan and heat on high before adding the chicken. Sear quickly on both sides to caramelize the chicken breast. Finish cooking in a preheated 300-degree oven. For skewers, cut the chicken into long tenders before marinating.

# Beef-cake Marinade

¼ cup Worcestershire sauce
¼ cup olive oil
3 cloves crushed garlic
1 tsp. Montreal Steak Seasoning

Combine all ingredients in a bowl until blended. Pour over hunky slabs of steak and let marinate, turning occasionally. Cook on a barbecue or sear on a stove-top pan until caramelized, then finish in the oven. Serve with your favorite vegetables.

# Meaty Meatballs w/Marinara Sauce

## Marinara Sauce

32 oz. tomato sauce
1 onion, cut in half with root intact, skin removed
¼ cup butter

This versatile sauce is simply the most delicious base for lasagna, spaghetti sauce, meatballs, and pizza sauce. It can be dolled up with fresh or dried herbs, red pepper flakes, chèvre, etc.

Empty one can of plain tomato sauce into a pot with a lid. Cut the onion in half but leave the root attached. Add it and ¼ cup butter to the pot. Heat to boiling and turn down immediately to medium low. Cover pot and continue to simmer for 5–10 minutes. Reduce heat further to lowest low and continue to heat until the onion wilts and falls apart. Toss the onion before serving.

## Meatballs

1 lb. ground beef or turkey
2 garlic cloves, minced
¼ tsp. pepper
¼ tsp. salt
¼ cup parsley
¼ cup bread crumbs
1 egg
¼ cup parmesan cheese

Mix all ingredients in a bowl until well blended. Roll into 2-ounce balls and place on a buttered cookie sheet or line it with parchment paper. Bake in a preheated 375-degree oven for approximately 12 minutes. Do not overcook. To use as an appetizer, roll the meatballs into 1-ounce rounds and bake for approximately 10 minutes. Skewer onto soaked bamboo skewers and serve with warm marinara sauce for dipping. Once prepared these meatballs can be frozen and reheated as needed.

# Creamy Sizzling Turkey Burgers

16 oz. ground turkey
½ tsp. Worcestershire sauce
½ tsp. pepper
½ tsp. seasoned salt
1½ oz. blue cheese
Avocado slices

The blue cheese in these burgers makes them drip with juicy goodness. Mix all ingredients in a bowl then form into four patties. Barbecue or pan sear on each side to color then finish in a 350-degree oven. Serve on your favorite buns and garnish with avocado slices.

# Succulent Chicken Salad Croissandwiches

1 tbsp. butter
½ yellow onion, finely chopped
½ apple, peeled and finely chopped
¼ cup chopped walnuts
2 cooked skinless chicken breasts, cubed
1–2 tbsp. mayonnaise
Salt and pepper to taste

Sauté chopped onion in butter until caramelized, being careful not to burn the onions. Cool before adding them to remaining ingredients in a large bowl. Fold until blended. Serve on fresh croissants with sliced tomato and arugula.

# Hot & Spicy Coleslaw

½ cup rice vinegar
2 tbsp. cane or refined white sugar
2 tbsp. grated fresh ginger (or 1 tsp. ground ginger)
½ tsp. salt
¾ tsp. crushed red pepper

Whisk above ingredients until combined and set aside.

3 cups shredded green cabbage
1 cup shredded red cabbage
1 large carrot, coarsely chopped
2 green onions, thinly sliced
¼ cup fresh parsley or cilantro

Place vegetables in a large bowl once shredded and chopped. Add enough dressing to coat. Let sit for an hour before serving. Keeps for 2–3 days but needs to be drained daily so it doesn't get soggy.

# Rapini & Bok Choy with Oyster Sauce

½ cup oyster sauce
¼ cup sesame oil
¼ tsp. black pepper
1 clove of garlic, minced
1 bunch rapini
1 bunch bok choy

Steam the rapini until just cooked and set aside. Cut the bulbous bottom off the bok choy and set aside. Combine oyster sauce, sesame oil, black pepper, and garlic in a bowl. Heat a frying pan on high and add the sauce mixture. When it is heated through, add the rapini and bok choy and stir until coated. Reduce heat and cook until tender.

## Secret Satay Sauce

½ cup roasted Spanish peanuts
1 tbsp. tamari
1 tbsp. soy sauce
1–2 tbsp. fresh lime juice
1–2 tbsp. maple syrup
2 tsp. chili sauce
1 clove garlic
1–4 tbsp. hot water

You can substitute ¼ cup unsweetened peanut butter for the fresh peanuts. Combine everything but the water in a food processor and mix until well blended and chunky. Add water one tablespoon at a time until all is blended and creamy. Serve as a topping to cooked soba noodles, baked chicken, or a dipping sauce for skewered chicken tenders, cooked green beans, or fried tofu chunks.

# Flash in the Pan Zucchini Rounds

2 big, long zucchini, washed and dried
¼ tsp. salt
¼ cup balsamic vinegar
1 tbsp. olive oil
Pepper to taste

Slice the zucchini in ¼-inch angled diagonal rounds. Lay out on a cookie sheet and sprinkle with salt on both sides. Let rest for about 20 minutes or until beads of sweat rise from the zucchini. Rinse the zucchini clean and pat dry. Heat olive oil and a dash of the balsamic vinegar in a large fry pan until hot. Add the zucchini rounds and cook until lightly browned, turning all rounds to cook on the other side. Cook until tender. Once complete remove from heat and drizzle with remaining balsamic vinegar. If using a cheap balsamic vinegar, you can heat it in a small pot on high until boiling, then turn the heat to medium and cook until reduced in half.

## Carrot & Cauliflower Sauté

3 tbsp. butter
1 onion, peeled and chopped
3 tomatoes
1 tbsp. garam masala
3 large carrots
1 head of cauliflower
1 cup coconut milk

Clean and cut the cauliflower, peel and slice the carrots into rounds. Boil vegetables until just tender. Drain and set aside. Sauté the onion in butter. Add tomatoes and garam masala. Cook until tomato has turned to sauce. Purée sauce once cooked and return to pan. Add coconut milk and stir. Add vegetables to sauce and stir until well-coated.

# Quick & Easy Shortbread Cookies

1 lb. butter
1 cup icing sugar

Cream butter and icing sugar until fluffy.

3 cups all-purpose flour
½ cup cornstarch
1 tsp. vanilla

Sift flour and cornstarch together. Add to creamed butter and sugar gradually. Add vanilla.

Pass through cookie pump or add a bit more flour and pat on board and cut into shapes. Place on lightly greased cookie sheet and bake at 350 degrees for 10–15 minutes. Shortbread cookies should be light in color when finished. Do not overbake.

## Acknowledgments

Heartfelt thanks to Judy Shepard. Your kind words in a rejection letter helped inspire this novel. To Paul and Dawn who created the perfect atmosphere for it to come alive. You sure make it look easy. I am beyond grateful to Elaine Ash, the best editor a girl could hope for.